ALPHA DRAGON REBORN

SHIFTERS OF THE AEGIS 5

LEELA ASH
TABITHA ST. GEORGE

CONTENTS

*S*ome days, Savannah Dare loved her last name. Bold and confident, it radiated competence. A spy like her couldn't ask for a better way to introduce herself. "Dare. Savannah Dare," sounded a helluva lot like "Bond. James Bond."

Today, however, sipping an espresso in The Coffee Pot, she didn't feel anything like a movie star. Today, her stomach tied itself in knots. Every second, she fought the urge to pat the briefcase at her feet, to make sure that it – and the precious information it contained – was safe.

Todd will be here soon. Then I'll know for certain, whether I was followed.

She hadn't spotted a tail. Then again, she wasn't a Shifter. Shape changers knew each other at once. A spirit animal followed everyone, invisible to mortal eyes – but obvious to another Shifters. Though Savannah's parents were Bears, she hadn't inherited their preternatural genes. Kin, like her, were as mortal as any normal human. Blind to the supernatural creatures of this world.

In the end, she was reduced to studying the people

around her, looking for any hint of a Shifter nature. That homeless man wandering past the window, was he ugly enough to be a Rat? The guy in the sweaty running pants, ordering a large non-fat latte… Bear or just an athlete?

Then, the doorbell chimed. Another man entered – and answered her question immediately.

Todd Manning was a tower of muscle and masculine power. Six-foot-six with arms the size of barrels, he dwarfed that latte drinker.

Todd was a Bear. Savannah's handler, her liaison with the Shifter community.

And her lover.

Some day, that would come back and bite her on the ass. She knew it. No sane agent slept with their contact. But when those intense brown eyes swept over her body, when he praised her beauty in his rich, bass voice, she lost her heart. A Bear – a full Shifter – like her. *Her*, a mere Kin! Even if he hadn't been hot as hell, the honor alone would have won her over.

Which is completely messed up. You know that, right?

She did. Technically, Kin weren't inferior to Shifters. People said the 'right' things, the 'nice' things about how everyone was equal. Lies, all of it. The truth was much uglier. It lurked in the shadows, revealing itself in little slips. The disappointment in her parents' eyes when they introduced her as Kin. The speed with which Shifters lost interest in someone when they couldn't see a spirit animal. Kin were second-rate citizens in the Shifter world. Loved… but not respected.

Unless they worked hard to prove their worth, as she had.

Over the last three years, she'd infiltrated the Fangs of Apophis, a monstrous gang of Shifters who sought to domi-nate the world, both mortal and supernatural. Through kidnapping, extortion, murder, and bribery, they destroyed anyone who opposed them. Starting as a secretary to some lesser minion, Savannah had risen slowly through the deadly labyrinth of their ranks. Two years ago, she earned a place at Ormaz Corporation, their Los Angeles headquarters. Secretary, then assistant. Rising, her false 'loyalty' unquestioned, to serve greater masters.

Since her arrival at Ormaz, Todd had been at her side. Well, in her shadow. Collecting information from her. Passing on requests from the Shifters who opposed the Fangs. Important people, like Brandon Lorde, the Alpha of the First Flight of Dragons.

And on the nights when she could slip away, Todd joined her. Making her feel important, *feminine*, in a way her work could never do.

Today's meeting brought no such pleasure. No surprise. She was way off script – and Todd didn't like it when things didn't go according to plan. Nervous and angry, her handler sipped his coffee for five minutes before he joined her. He scanned the street and coffee bar, judging each stranger, weighing them. Savannah tensed. If he turned around and left without speaking to her, it meant the game was up. The Fangs had followed her. Her cover was blown.

To her relief, Todd finally brought his coffee over to her corner table. "Why are you here?" he hissed.

"I need to talk to you."

Once more, his eyes flickered around the room, wary and hostile. "If the Fangs see you with me, a Shifter, you're dead."

As if she didn't know that! Still, he *was* her lover. He had a right to worry. Plus, Bears, more than any other Kind, fixated on their loved ones and family. Dragons valued honor too, Rats... survival, Wolves... freedom. For Bears, family was their whole existence.

"I'll be quick." She placed the slender briefcase on the

table and pushed it toward him. "I found out what happened to Aaron Cole."

That caught his attention. Todd pulled the case close, one huge mitt of a hand lain possessively across it. "The Dragon from the First Flight who went missing?"

"Yes. He's dead."

The Bear took the news in with a surprising lack of shock. "How?"

"The Fangs have figured out a way to enchant Dragons. To lull them into, well, a waking sleep. They just stand there and don't defend themselves."

Todd shrugged. A casual dismissal that stung like a slap. "We already know that. They've used it against the First Flight."

Somehow, he always made her feel stupid, like an over-eager schoolgirl who didn't know half as much as she thought she did. Ignoring the heat that flooded her cheeks, Savannah pressed on. "This is different. They used a spirit trap against the First Flight. A magical artifact they found in Greece. The Fangs only have one – and it can only snare one Dragon. This is much worse. It's a song. Any Dragon who hears it is mesmerized."

Now, his lips pinched. *Now,* he understood why she had to break protocol and talk to him. "That could take out an entire Flight in one go."

The idea was horrifying. Shifters' most powerful defenders... destroyed by one song. Eyes burning with conviction, she leaned across the table. "I think I have a lead on this. The notes I found suggested that a Witch Hare called Mariset oversees this research. If I can find out more about her, I can–"

"No." Todd's growl of disapproval was sharp and quick.

Just like a Bear! Protect your lover, no matter what. He probably didn't even realize how often he tried to smother her.

But nothing, not even an upset Bear, was chasing her off this trail. "If I can get a sample of this music, our Hares can–"

"No! It's too dangerous. We know this Mariset. She serves one of the senior Fangs, a Worm named Alester."

Alester, hmm? Good to know. If only her handler wasn't working himself into a fit over this. "Todd, listen." Gently, she took his big hand in her two small ones. "I know you want to protect me, but this is something I have to do, no matter how dangerous it is."

He didn't pull away but he didn't soften either. Instead, his lip curled back in a sneer. "Do you honestly think the Fangs would allow information like this to fall into the hands of a mere secretary? Savannah, you're nobody. You're nothing."

She knew he didn't mean that, not the way it sounded. *You're not a high-ranking Fang* was more accurate. Still, it hurt. How could he be so careless with his words?

And so oblivious to the pain they caused? Todd bulldozed on as if nothing had happened. "Drop this matter. We'll have someone else investigate. Someone who's infiltrated more deeply than you have."

There were other Shifter spies working secretly beside her? Maybe that should have been a relief; not everything rested upon her shoulders. But it hurt.

And, after today, it wasn't believable. "I've got other news. I just got a promotion. There's a new 'master' coming to Ormaz. Jordan Beaumont. I'm going to be his administrative assistant."

A position that would give her access to some of the most sensitive information flowing through the Fangs. Such a breakthrough should have delighted her handler – but it didn't. Todd simply scowled. "Haven't heard of this guy before."

Another cup of cold water dumped on her pride. Well,

she wouldn't let some morose Bear bring her down. If she needed to spell out how big this was, then so be it! "Apparently, he's old. Like, really old. Maybe one of the Fangs' first members. He's been 'out of touch' for a long time, though, and I've been warned that I'll need to help bring him up to speed."

"'Out of touch'?" Todd huffed. "Where the hell has he been?"

"That's what I want to find out. Among other things."

Like how, exactly, the Fangs had killed Aaron Cole. And why they hadn't unleashed this new weapon on other Dragons.

Slowly, her lover nodded. "I think you're right. Working with this Beaumont could give you access to critical information."

That was the odd thing about Todd. Normally, he displayed all the intense, over-the-top, protective urges of a Bear. Once he'd decided a risk was worthwhile, however, he put his feelings behind him. Something her parents – and most Bears – could never do.

Which is probably why he's my handler and they're not!

Frankly, the last thing she needed was to have a man fussing over the risks she took. Nobody ever said undercover work would be safe! "Glad we're on the same page. I should get back to work before they notice I'm gone. Next report goes to the usual drop?"

"Yes. Oh, and any word on the Darkborn situation?"

The Darkborn were the one threat that both Shifters and Fangs agreed on. Spirits from the Other Side, a world of magic, they served the demon lord Nemagorix. Ancient shamans had bound Nemagorix in the Other Side, using a relic they called the Aegis. But no prison lasted forever. Nemagorix was breaking free and sought a gate back to mortal realms.

Back when Savannah entered the ranks of the Fangs, no

one knew about this demon or the threat it posed to the world. The Fangs were Enemy #1... until the First Flight learned that not all Fangs were truly Fangs. Darkborn could possess both animals and spirts. They'd taken over senior Fangs, turned that corrupt organization to their own ends. When the Fangs learned about this betrayal, it unleashed a bloody purge. No one, not even the most gifted Hare, could detect a Darkborn when it hid within a Shifter's body.

Witch hunts and paranoia had become a way of life among the Fangs. No one was safe. Anyone could be a Darkborn's pawn.

As a lowly secretary, the worst of those purges had passed Savannah, high overhead. That would change, now that she served a powerful master.

"No major news, no," she told Todd. "Security has been insanely high ever since the Fangs learned that many of their leaders were possessed. But other than rampant fear and random purges, they haven't figured out how to deal with this."

"What about the Aegis?"

"Nothing." She hadn't heard a peep about the Shifters' great hope. Once lost, the Aegis was back in good hands. An informal group, the Shifters of the Aegis, watched over it. But no one had any idea how to actually use the Aegis to bind Nemagorix. "The Fangs would like to steal it but can't figure out how. It's too well protected."

"Good." With a curt nod, he rose to his feet with her briefcase. "Looking forward to your next report."

Just like that, the meeting was over. Disappointment stung Savannah as her lover turned to go. "Todd?"

"Yes?"

"Is there any chance we could... you know... see each other soon?"

"I don't think that's wise. A promotion means more scrutiny for you."

True. Being alone, though, was a heavy price to pay.

Without another word, he walked off. Leaving her with a cold cup of coffee and an ache in her heart.

He's right. If the Fangs knew I had a Bear lover, they'd kill me.

True. Yet, the danger hadn't stopped him in the past. Had something changed? Did he not find her attractive anymore?

Silly. Savannah pushed her cup – and her foolish emotions – aside. She was a spy, an undercover operative for the Shifters of the Aegis and the First Flight. Emotion had no place in her life.

Or so she told herself, over and over, as she trudged out the door and back into the heart of the battle.

CHAPTER 2

The Fangs of Apophis weren't exactly known for being supportive, caring employers. Treachery and greed drenched every part of the organization, from the powerful Worms of its Inner Council, all the way down to the janitorial staff. So, Savannah wasn't at all surprised to find that her sudden promotion set off a tidal wave of seething resentment.

None of the other secretaries spoke to her as she slipped back to her desk, one of a dozen in the 'General Assistants' room. No questions, no greetings… not even a catty remark. Just cold stares and pinched lips. Every time she glanced up from her computer, she found one of her co-workers glaring at her. Each one dropped their eyes, though, as soon as Savannah looked their way.

Probably wondering who they need to sleep with to get a promotion.

She endured their cold stares for a couple hours, until a series of sharp, hard 'clacks' announced the arrival of Lara Pearl. Six-inch, blood-red stiletto heels rapped the marble floor as she swept in, her lean body wrapped in the red silk embrace of Giorgio Armani's latest creation. Eddy Adams ruled Ormaz Corp., this particular nest of Fangs – and Lara was his personal assistant. For mere secretaries like Savannah, she was a goddess. Every eye, no matter how envious, dropped reverently as she approached.

"Miss Doucette."

After three years undercover, that fake name felt as real to Savannah as her own. "Yes, Miss Pearl?"

"Time to move to your new office." Her supervisor's eyes swept across the other secretaries, bright with disdain. "I wouldn't bother saying goodbye to anyone. Losers like these would only hold you back."

Good thing I never made any friends here, Savannah thought as she grabbed her purse and rose to follow Lara. *I wouldn't have any left by the time she got done!*

Lara didn't say another word until the elevator doors closed behind them. Then, as they glided skyward, she turned and raked Savannah up and down with bitter, sharp disdain. Her eyes paused on her black cashmere top and floral print dress.

"Dolce and Gabbana?"

"Yes." Four paychecks went into that dress – but it made a statement.

"Good. Those shoes are some off the rack little horrors, though."

"Well, yes, but I can't afford to…"

"Don't make excuses," Lara snapped. "Just fix the problem. At our level, details matter. Combining a designer dress with cheap knock-off accessories makes you look like a fool."

"Understood."

'Miss Doucette' was a fake, a persona used to infiltrate the Fangs. Yet, Savannah felt her cheeks sting under the lash of Lara's words.

"Good. Then, let's have a look at your face."

Wonderful. What's wrong with me now?

Lara heaved a sigh. "Make up is competent and under-stated – though very conservative. I myself favor brighter colors. They demonstrate strength. Your lipstick shrieks, 'I'm a simpering git. Ignore me.'"

"Isn't that what my master is going to want?"

Delighted, the cruel woman smiled. "Good question, Miss Doucette. That's precisely what you *should* be asking – and why you got promoted over those posers in the secretarial pool. From now on, your master is your god. Your only goal is to please him and serve him. You need to review yourself, continually. Examine every aspect of your dress, figure, and behavior, and ask yourself 'Is this what he wants?'"

It took all of Savannah's self-control to keep her expression neutral during that vile outburst. But she was a professional. In the end, she simply ducked her head and said, "Thank you for that advice, ma'am."

"Oh, I'm not done. Normally, I'd send you down to Tran Salon for a complete make-over."

"What's wrong with my hair?" Thick, full, and luscious, it fell, in rich brown waves, halfway down her back. Every man she met adored it!

Lara didn't. "First, it's out of style. Too feminine."

Savannah hadn't realized that was a problem in women's haircuts...

"Second, the color bores me to tears." Her supervisor's hair was dyed black with purple highlights. "Personally, I think you'd do better in canary yellow. Crop it off, shave the sides, and volumize the top."

That would certainly take care of the too-feminine 'problem.'

"Thank you for your advice, ma'am. I'll..."

"You'll ignore me – if you're smart," Lara countered. "I'm not your master. Remember: His opinion is all that matters.

And you're lucky. Your master is very old-fashioned. He probably won't think you're frumpy at all."

A loud ding announced their arrival. Still reeling from Lara's critiques, Savannah stepped out of the elevator.

Into a world of cold beauty.

Black slate corridors stretched to the left and right. Every interior wall was covered with the latest modern art. All exteriors were glass, offering breath-taking views across the city and out toward the ocean. Silvery steel and ebony stone set the tone. Other than the paintings, not a drop of color breathed life into this place. It was a cold, elegant mausoleum.

"This way."

Lara escorted her to a suite of rooms at the end of the corridor.

Corner office, facing the ocean. A testament to my boss' importance.

A senior Fang would expect no less.

"Your desk." Glass and steel, it radiated competence and power. "Your master's office is there. Conference room. Restroom." Private bathroom, no less! And complete with a stone-floored shower! "Lounge."

A conference room *and* a lounge? The furniture in that last room surprised her. Comfortable chairs, a tv, and a sleek chaise lounge long enough to sleep on. "Is this where I'll take my lunches?"

Lara laughed, a sound half cackle, half snort of disbelief. "Oh heavens, no. There's a staff room at the end of the hall. No master wants to see his assistant eat – or smell the stench of her meal."

"All right." Maybe the master slept here when he worked late? Savannah began to turn away when the other woman snickered.

"You really don't understand, do you?"

Slowly, she shook her head.

"Miss Doucette, an assistant's job is to take care of her master's needs. *All* of his needs."

A chill swept over her as the implication of that hit her. "You don't mean… you can't…"

"Oh, I do!" The glint in Lara's eye betrayed how much she was enjoying Savannah's shock. "Is that a problem? Please tell me you're not a virgin."

"No, but…"

"But you're shy?" Lara simpered. "You have a boyfriend that you – mistakenly – think is more important than your master?"

Todd. If she betrayed him, she would never be able to look him in the eye again. No job was worth such a sacrifice!

Not even one that saves lives? If Nemagorix breaks into this world again, thousands of people will die.

Her boss' words cut through that pregnant silence. "Miss Doucette, if you can't satisfy *all* of your master's desires, speak up now."

Savannah licked her lips. "I'll lose the job, won't I?"

"Of course. Trust me, though." Lara leaned close, letting the scent of her Chanel perfume waft over the brown-haired Kin. "Getting banished back to the secretarial pool is a *lot* better than disappointing your master. You know who we are. The Fangs do *not* handle disappointment well."

Could she sleep with some monster? Even to save lives?

No. But…

Maybe I won't have to face that risk – if I move fast. Get into their computer system, get the info we need, then get out.

Back to Todd, and safety.

She could do that. *And* keep her honor intact.

"Miss Doucette? Your answer?"

Savannah straightened her shoulders and met the awful

woman's gaze straight on. "There's no problem, ma'am. I'll do whatever's necessary."

"Good." To her surprise, Lara seemed genuinely relieved. "It would be difficult to replace you on such short notice. Worse, that failure would reflect badly on me."

Well, then, you should have asked if I minded adding 'prostitute' to my resume.

How horrible was it that Lara assumed no woman who worked for the Fangs would flinch at such a request?

Down the hallway, the soft chime of the elevator's bell announced new arrivals.

"Show time," Lara hissed as Savannah's stomach churned. "Stand behind the desk. It'll hide those hideous shoes. And stop by payroll on your way out. I'll approve an advance on your next check. Can't have you embarrassing yourself."

Meek and submissive – on the outside, anyway – she obeyed, and prepared to meet her master.

Her 'god.'

Two men stepped through the doorway. One, she knew.

A Wolf by birth, Eddy Adams was the CEO of Ormaz. He ruled this 'Pack' with an iron-will. Ruthless, he was as comfortable ordering a murder as a pizza. A Kin-woman like her couldn't see his Wolf, his Shifter soul. Yet, his clothes gave away his Kind: silken shirt and blazer… over jeans and Nike sneakers. No Wolf obeyed rules. Especially not one as powerful as Adams.

Today, though, something was wrong. Savannah could sense it. In the rapid patter that spilled out of Eddy – as if the thought of silence frightened him. In the fake smile plastered across his face and the false humor that 'brightened' his voice.

Unthinkable though it was, Eddy Adams was afraid. Of the man beside him.

Her master. Her 'god.'

He stepped in the doorway behind Adams and surveyed his new office. At the first touch of his eyes, Savannah froze like a deer in headlights.

Tall and broad shouldered, he truly looked like one of the old Greek gods. Hair as black as a raven's wing, a strong 'Roman' nose, sharp cheekbones. Bright, intelligent green eyes, like two chips of emerald, weighed his new domain. Though he lacked a Bear's muscular strength, he radiated authority. His confidence, his power, cowed all around him. This was a king, a man who demanded – and expected – obedience.

What Kind is he?

Not a Rat or a Bear, obviously. He was too handsome for the one Kind and not burly enough for the second. No Hare exuded such complete and total confidence. A Wolf, perhaps? But his blue silk suit and slacks, the crisp sweep of his hair, argued against that. Wolves always looked a little wild, no matter how hard they struggled to 'clean up.'

Which meant only one thing. Savannah's heart began to race at the thought.

He was a Worm. A fallen Dragon. The worst of the worst. A monster that had chewed his own wings off in a fit of madness.

Could she deceive such a creature? Could her acting, her lies, withstand a tainted Dragon's piercing study?

Or... perhaps she didn't need to. Hare, Rat, Wolf, Bear, and Dragon were the five most common Kinds of Shifters. Others existed, however. Why, just recently, a Chimera joined the Shifters of the Aegis, a Kind she'd never even heard of. For all she knew, her master was one of those. Strange, unusual...

...but not as terrifying as a Worm.

"Good afternoon, Mr. Adams," Lara purred.

"Miss Pearl. Allow me to introduce the newest addition to our team: Jordan Beaumont."

Under the newcomer's lordly scrutiny, even Lara quailed. "It's an honor to meet you, sir. This is Savannah Doucette, your assistant."

Now, those piercing eyes turned on her, and Savannah felt her lips grow dry. "An honor, sir," she murmured, unconsciously mimicking her boss' words.

Eddy's smile dimmed. "Hell, Pearl, couldn't you find anyone a bit more glamorous? What the hell is that hairstyle even called?"

Her new master spoke before Lara could even open her mouth. "I would call it 'beautiful.'"

Pride and fear warred in her heart. He liked her.

Let's hope he doesn't like me enough to demand 'other' services...

Eddy giggled, a nervous sound that shocked both women. "Hey, if you dig it, that's all that matters. Am I right?"

Jordan ignored him. A moment later, the view over the city drew his attention, freeing Savannah from the iron grasp of his interest. "I should like some coffee," he said as he strolled toward the conference room.

Not the lounge. Good. And coffee was the safest, simplest request he could make. "How do you take yours, sir?"

"Black."

Of course.

"Cream and two sugars for me," Eddy added. "Pearl, leave us."

Lara's presence was meager comfort, yet Savannah regretted seeing her leave. Quickly, she busied herself making coffee as the two men settled into the conference room. Eddy did most of the talking, filling the silence with the Fangs' equivalent of small talk. Who disrespected him.

Who he'd had killed or beat up. How many Rats he'd managed to blackmail into helping the Fangs.

She kept half an ear on that talk as she made the coffee. You never know when there'd be a vital bit of information floating in the revolting stew of boasts and threats (what passed for 'conversation' among the Fangs). Eddy's prattle didn't slow, even when she stepped between them, carrying their drinks.

Maybe it was the slate floor, so slick and strange. Maybe her shoes truly were 'cheap knockoffs.' But as she bent to set the coffee on the table, Savannah felt one heel twist.

Time slowed, like a scene from a horror movie, as the tray she held tilted wildly. She saw the steaming cups slide… hit the edge of the tray… and go tumbling off. One bounced across the glass table, scattering its hot contents over the clear surface. The other cracked against the table's edge and dumped its scalding contents onto Eddy's knee.

The Wolf's scream of pain and outrage yanked the world back into focus. Savannah flinched as he bolted to his feet and cocked his hand back. "You *stupid* bitch!"

With his full strength, he slapped her.

Or rather, he tried.

But, as Eddy swung, Jordan's hand shot out too. He caught the Wolf's wrist in an iron grasp, freezing him in place before he could lay a finger on her.

"You don't touch her," was all her master said. Cool and unperturbed, despite the coffee that had sprayed everywhere.

"She needs to be taught a lesson!" the Wolf snarled. "She…"

Jordan's fingers tightened and the rest of that sentence disappeared in a squeal of pain. And suddenly, his calm demeanor vanished. Light flared in his eyes, a blood-red gleam that turned his handsome features demonic.

"My assistant is *my* property!" he snarled. "You *never* touch *my* property!"

Heart beating wildly, Savannah knelt between them and dropped her eyes, every inch the submissive minion. Even Eddy, the supposed 'Alpha' of Ormaz, quailed. "Sorry," he muttered. "Sorry. It won't happen again."

"No, it will not." The light faded as Jordan released the Wolf's hand. "Now, leave us. I have nothing more to say to you."

Like a chastised puppy, Eddy Adams did exactly that. As he scurried away, Savannah struggled to make sense out of the scene.

Who is this guy? Eddy is a high-ranking Fang and he just... just...

Just saved her from getting beaten up.

Probably because he wanted to do it himself. Kneeling, head lowered, she waited to learn her fate and punishment.

"Clean this up." Calm once more, no one would ever suspect the rage that had seized him only a moment before. "Then bring me another cup of coffee in my office. I have a lot of work to do."

Without another word, her master left.

Leaving her relieved – and confused.

Who the hell was Jordan Beaumont? And what would he demand of her?

CHAPTER 3

*A*fternoon and evening passed in a whirlwind. Jordan Beaumont wasn't joking when he said he had a ton of work. For hours, Savannah labored beside him. Gathering reports. Mailing queries to various spies and agents. Crawling through scholarly articles on the archeology of the American Southwest.

After just one afternoon, she already knew where his true interest lay: her 'master' sought more information on the Aegis. He had thick files on the Shifters of the Aegis, the four men who had been 'claimed' by the relic. Casey Briggs, a Dragon from the Flight of the Snows. Lucas Clay, lone Wolf. Rex Fairburn, Bear and local real estate developer. Griffin Davis, Chimera. Jordan dug through volumes of data, gathering every scrap of information on these people. Searching endlessly for some common thread. Some elusive quality they all shared.

Something that made the Aegis choose them, out of all men.

Savannah had a folder of her own. It held the names of

the spies who watched these men, and what the Fangs had learned.

Todd will have to be careful using this. I can't risk blowing my cover. But the Shifters of the Aegis are our only hope, the key to stopping Nemagorix. Protecting them is my most important duty.

That thought made her smile. Every one of the Aegis' chosen was a powerful Shifter. Some of the greatest warriors in the world. The idea that she, a mere Kin, might protect them was ludicrous.

Unless you remember that you can't fight what you don't see. My job is to reveal their enemies to them.

IN ANY NORMAL OFFICE, TODAY WOULD HAVE BEEN A PLEASANT, busy day. Ormaz Corp., however, was anything but normal. The absolute power that a Fang master enjoyed cast a dark shadow over Savannah. A fear, a cold, creeping dread that, at any moment, she might look up and find Jordan Beaumont watching. Hungry. Lusting after her. Ready to demand the 'services' that the masters expected of their servants.

At 7:30 pm, Jordan stepped into his doorway. Immediately, Savannah snapped to attention. "Yes, master? How may I serve?"

Standard language for a minion in the Fangs, yet he winced. "I dislike that term. 'Mr. Beaumont' will suffice."

"Yes, mmm… Mister Beaumont." A three-year habit was hard to break!

"It's late. I lost track of time and for that, I apologize."

He… what? Savannah squinted at him, unsure if this was a trick. Fangs of Apophis didn't apologize. Especially not over something so trivial.

"I'm sure you're quite exhausted. You may go now. We'll pick up again tomorrow morning at 8:30."

While she hesitated, waiting for the trap to spring, he returned to his office.

And that was it. No demand that she kneel and pleasure him. No unwanted touches or lewd comments. Cold and distant though he was, Jordan remained a gentleman.

Something she'd *never* met in these halls!

Without a word, she gathered her belongings and went home.

Baths were the best remedy for stress. Soaking in a hot tub, head propped up by a neck pillow, Savannah closed her eyes. Water, warm and peaceful, lapped against her bare skin. Slowly, her muscles softened as the day's tension drained away. With each deep breath, she inhaled the scent of sweet lavender.

Bliss… heaven… peace… until another scent wove its way into the floral aroma.

Rot. A chill breeze washed over her, rich with the stench of mold and damp.

Savannah's eyes snapped open.

Her bathroom had vanished. Only the tub remained, surrounded by dark mist. A bright spotlight burned down from the mist, creating a small circle of light around it. The only light in this twilight.

What the hell…?

A moment later, she understood.

This is a dream. I fell asleep in the tub.

Normally, that thought alone would wake her. This time, though, the dream persisted.

Not the first time I've done this. Fortunately my inflatable pillow will keep my nose above water!

This particular dream seemed determined to slip into a nightmare. Out in the darkness, water dripped. Another cold breeze whispered by, and she marveled at the sharp details. The faint scent of decay. The goosebumps that rose on her arms. Everything was as clear as real life.

Somewhere in the distance, someone spoke. "Help me."

Man, woman, child, or thing, she couldn't tell. "Hello?"

"Help me. Please."

Walk out into that eerie, echoing darkness?

Why not? I'm not a coward in real life – and I'm sure as hell not going to dream about being chicken.

Slippers and a white cotton robe lay beside the tub. She slid into them and strode confidently out into the darkness.

Mist closed around her, rank and clinging. A faint luminescence burned within it that let her see vague shapes. Not that there was much to look at. Ground beneath her feet, hard and smooth, almost like pavement. Gradually, sounds whispered in, surrounding her. Women weeping. Harsh laughter. Screams. Always distant and muffled, as if they echoed across a huge abyss.

"Help me."

Still, that voice led her on through the night, sad and despairing.

A door loomed out of the mist. Attached to nothing, it stood, the lone speck of matter in this emptiness.

At least my dream makes it clear where I'm supposed to go!

Smiling, she opened it.

A bedroom lay on the other side. Vaguely, she noticed tapestries, a canopy bed...

With two people in it, making love. A man and a woman wrapped in each other's arms, locked in passion. Embarrassed by her own dream, Savannah began to back out quietly. As she did, the woman's mouth popped open.

"Oh!" she shrieked. "It's you!" Shoving the man aside, the stranger snatched up her sheets and clutched them to her chest. "I can explain! I swear! This isn't what it looks like!"

What was she supposed to say to that? Annoyed by her own silly dream, Savannah sighed…

…then jumped when a man spoke at her elbow. "That's what they *always* say. And yet, it *is* exactly what it looks like. Every time."

Jordan Beaumont, her 'master', stood behind her. Staring at the tryst before them with dull displeasure. "At least my subconscious had the courtesy, this time, to remind me that all women are the same. Treacherous. Deceitful."

"Hah!" The snort escaped Savannah before she could stop it. "A Fang of Apophis calling other people 'treacherous'! That's rich!"

"You're a Fang too."

"Pfft! No, I'm not. I'm spying for the First Flight." It was a dream, after all. No harm in being honest.

Jordan pursed his lips. "Strange. Why would I think that of you?"

Speaking of strange… why the hell was she dreaming about this guy?

All afternoon, I'm terrified that he's going to demand I have sex with him. Then, the minute I fall asleep, he's here?

In all his glory. Somehow, her subconscious had kept every detail of him. Everything she'd tried to forget. Physically, Jordan was perfect. Broad cheeks, sleek black hair, emerald eyes. Powerful muscles playing beneath his silken shirt. Yet, his body, delicious as it was, was only half of his appeal. Raw masculinity radiated from him. It simmered in his unflinching visage, promising that he would always get what he desired. It smoldered in the lordly way he surveyed the world around him, ready to defeat anyone who might challenge him.

This was an Alpha. A man with not the slightest shred of softness in him. Faced with his domineering aura, Savannah felt something stir inside her. Something feminine, and hungry.

And unwanted.

Seriously? I worry about this guy raping me all day long. Now I want to jump his bones?

Well… yes. Consent changed everything. Jordan Beaumont was a spectacular man. Could she blame herself for wanting him?

This was a dream after all, no matter how real it felt. She couldn't blame herself for her dreams.

Right?

"Help me."

A corridor faded into view around them, edged with stone walls like a castle. Open doors marched down its length and from somewhere near its end, that plaintive voice begged once more.

"What's that?" she asked.

"What's what?"

He couldn't hear that? "Look, Mr. Beaumont…" Even in her dreams, she wasn't daring enough to call him by his first name? That was *not* acceptable! "*Jordan*. I have a boyfriend, so I'm not sure I want to make love to you, even in my dreams. Plus, somebody's in trouble, and I need to go rescue them."

"Who said anything about sex?" Vague affront lit his eyes, as if he couldn't believe she'd walk away from him – even in a dream. But she did. Savannah trudged down the hall, heading for that plea for help.

Jordan followed, stewing silently. Every doorway revealed some new unpleasantness. A laughing young woman who crumbled into dust. Another lady, older, surrounded by four children in colonial garb. They, too, dissolved and blew away. Another door revealed a treasure vault, piled high with golden bars and gems. As they passed, all those riches melted like wax under the summer sun.

"So it is, always," he sighed. "Nothing lasts. Not love. Not family. Not art. Not riches. Nothing. The Abyss claims it all in the end."

"So what?"

Sharp and impertinent, her question shocked him. Jordan stared as if she were a tiny hamster which had suddenly grown fangs and bitten his finger off.

Good. Her family had never tolerated wallowing, and she didn't plan to start now. "Of course, nothing lasts forever. Life *is* change. That doesn't mean it's not worthwhile! You savor every moment, grieve your losses, and then find the strength to open your heart again. Because there *will* be an 'again.' Life is beautiful!"

"Life is a monotonous parade of boredom and sorrow," he grumbled.

"Well, then, you're doing it wrong." Five minutes ago, she hadn't dared to call him 'Jordan.' Now, faced with this self-indulgent angst, her annoyance gave her the courage to be honest with him. "Jordan, life should be wonderful."

"You don't understand," he huffed.

"I understand just fine. I'm the one who's happy, remember? Which sort of proves *you're* the one who doesn't get it."

"You are a mayfly!" he snapped. "A gnat whose life is crammed into one single day! I am ancient! You have no idea of the weight of time, how it…"

Savannah ignored him and stomped off. Somewhere, somebody needed saving. It was time she did that – and got out of this silly dream.

A heavy oak door lay at the end of the hall. From behind it, her voice whispered once more. "Help me."

She tried the handle. It was locked. "Hello?"

Jordan trotted up behind her, simmering with annoyance. "You are not listening."

"No, I'm not. Because life is wonderful, and you're

complaining... *complaining!* – that you have too much of it. Can you get this door open?"

"What?" His fierce scowl turned on the innocent door. "Why?"

"Because I can hear someone calling for help from behind it, and it's locked. To me, anyway."

He reached for the doorknob, but as his fingers brushed it, he snatched his hand back, hissing in pain.

Once more, the voice spoke. Louder, and now clearly male. "Show her."

What a weird dream! Jordan stared at the door with open loathing until Savannah tapped his arm. "I don't think I'm going to wake up until you do what it says, so...."

"*You* will wake up?" he scoffed. Teeth gritted, he wrapped his fingers around the knob. This time, the door opened smoothly.

A shattered crystal goblet lay on the floor. Beside it, a pile of rust that might once have been a dagger. Beyond them, rose an enormous pile of bones. Monstrously large, like the remains of a dinosaur.

Or a Dragon...

Cautiously, Savannah inched forward. The hem of her robe brushed against the rust and sent it spilling across the floor. Jordan joined her, his face bleak with agony.

"You see? There is nothing."

Without warning, a wall of emotion crashed down upon her. Weariness, a soul-killing fatigue that destroyed the will. Infinite boredom, the certain knowledge that there was nothing in the world she had not already seen. Nothing new, nothing beautiful. Nothing worth living for. Woven through that, like the scent of a rotting corpse, lay despair. She was appalling, a monster. An abomination that no one could ever love.

No, not *her*. The feelings that threatened to drown her were strange, alien.

They're his, not mine.

Wincing from the pain of those borrowed emotions, Savannah staggered. Neither joy nor satisfaction brightened Jordan's eyes as he murmured, "Now, you see. Now, you understand."

Seeing was one thing – surrendering was another. She was Bear Kin. Bears didn't give up, they didn't run. They stood their ground and protected their families. They *certainly* didn't allow self-pity to drag them under. Fists clenched, she fought back against the tide of misery.

Something moved among the bones, a tiny flicker of light. Savannah dropped to her knees.

A movement that Jordan assumed meant surrender. "Thus, all great dreams end, all delusions of love and honor."

Ignoring him, she pushed aside a pile of small bones. Beneath them, lay a glittering dragonfly. At first, she thought it a brooch. Its body seemed carved of emerald, its wings tiny sheets of alabaster. Yet, as she freed it, those delicate wings fluttered weakly.

"Look at this." Carefully, she scooped it into the palm of her hand. Cold radiated from it, the icy ache of deep winter. A chill that quickly vanished as she breathed upon its fragile body. Scales brightened and a cloud of minute sparkles glittered across them. Wings stretched, fanned. With two stiff legs, the little insect began to groom itself, wiping its gem-like eyes.

Jordan stared at it in disdain. "A bug? Is that what amazes you?"

"Life," she corrected him. "Life amazes me. When you look around, all you see is death and decay. Did you even notice this guy?"

"That *insect*. No, I did not notice such an insignificant thing."

"Hope and life are *never* pointless!" She breathed on it again, hoping that her body's warmth would comfort the little creature.

At the touch, its wings blurred into furious motion. The dragonfly rose into the air and buzzed about the gigantic skeleton. Motes of light danced in the air behind it, weaving bright streamers around the bones. It glittered, the one tiny speck of color in this gloomy underworld.

"You see?" she asked Jordan, chin raised in defiance.

The Fang only shook his head. "All I see is shame. A meaningless bug where there should be a magnificent Dragon. A shiny pebble where a mountain of strength and power ought to stand."

"Forget the 'shoulds' and 'ought tos.'" She placed a soft hand on his clenched fists. "The only thing that matters is what *is*. And that 'meaningless bug'? It exists. It's hope. It's the promise that things can still get better."

"You *believe* that." It was a statement, not a question. For the first time, a crack appeared in his stern, confident façade. Only a hairline fracture, but his face betrayed him. In the way his emerald eyes widened, and how his lips, full and strong, parted. He leaned in, as if her faith was a magnet reeling him closer.

"I do." This near, she felt the heat of his body. Every delectable detail on full display. Hair black as night, sweeping past those high, aristocratic cheekbones. The faint shadow of a beard that gave a rakish cast to his chin. Piercing green eyes, as proud and fierce as a hawk's.

Jordan Beaumont was the most delicious man she'd ever seen. Or, well, dreamed about.

He also wasn't a man who doubted himself. Sensing her

arousal, he leaned down and kissed her; his lips claiming hers. No permission need be asked.

That touch, so enticing, so unexpected, sent a charge tingling down her spine. Everything faded away except the moment. Those lips, warm, open, pressed against hers. The strength of his arm drawing her near, declaring her his own. The faint, male musk of his body. Her body came alive. Heat flashed through her and a fire, a hunger, woke within her.

Not until that kiss broke could she think again. Then, the first nagging doubt clawed at her bliss.

Todd. She had a boyfriend – and he wasn't Jordan Beaumont.

"I shouldn't…," she whispered, and her heart ached at that refusal.

Jordan simply chuckled. "I will not be denied by my own dream. If I am going to torment myself with vain hopes, then I deserve to enjoy vain pleasures."

What was he babbling about? *His* dream? It was hers!

Though… her imaginary boss raised a good point: this wasn't real. You couldn't blame a woman for her dreams, could you? It wasn't unfaithful to have a nocturnal fantasy about her hot (if villainous) 'master.' In fact, if she were honest, Savannah knew exactly why this was happening.

Todd is so distracted. Sex seems like a chore to him, not an act of love. It's been that way for a year and a half now.

A scary thought, given that they'd only been together for two years.

I'm depressed. I don't feel sexy, I don't feel like a woman. Is it really a shock that I'm having erotic dreams?

No, it wasn't. And if this released her pent-up frustrations… Why, it might actually help her *real* relationship.

So, screw it. I'm doing this.

Around them, bones and darkness vanished. In their place,

a bed appeared. Broad and welcoming, draped by lace curtains. A room faded in too. Thick Persian rugs underfoot, tapestries lining stone walls. Glass doors ran along one wall. Open now, they offered breath-taking views of snow-covered Alps.

Jordan nodded. "Much better."

Without warning, muscled arms scooped her into the air. Savannah gave a startled gasp… then flushed with pleasure as he strode toward the bed. Nestled in his embrace, she felt a scandalous, decadent pleasure. She was his captive, his prize.

She couldn't have denied him, even if she wished.

With ease, he carried her to the bed, laying her down gently among its soft cotton pillows. The white robe she wore offered little resistance to his advances. One tug released the loose knot of its woven belt. Jordan settled on the bed next to her. Gently, he stroked her chin. Then, his hand glided lower, along the curve of her throat. A shiver of longing trembled through her at that touch. His fingers caught the edge of her robe. Yet, instead of tearing it off, they caressed. Sliding the robe open just enough to reveal the swell between her breasts. Lower still. One fold of cloth slipped over her hip, revealing the curves of her buttocks and thigh. Its twin, however, demurely covered her sex. Leaving the last of her mysteries still hidden from his view.

Emerald eyes gleamed, the shadow of a smile crossed his lips and Jordan drank in the sight of her.

Now, his mask of self-control fell away to reveal the hunger that lay beneath. He did not touch her, not with his hands. Only his eyes devoured her. Tasting the curls of her long brown hair and tan skin. His breath deepened as his gaze lingered on her breasts, half hidden.

Some small, silly voice urged her to *do* something to please him.

But she didn't need to *do* anything. The sight of her pleased him.

How long had it been since a man watched her with such open, naked hunger? The mere sight of her intoxicated him, and Savannah let her lover drink his fill, reveling in the sense of feminine power that his adoration awoke in her. His was the need of a starving man, and she was the feast he desired. The yearning within her blazed under the fire of his eyes.

Jordan trailed a finger down the crevice between her breasts. His touch stirred her robe and her nipples stiffened as rough cotton whispered across them. Slowly, he bent, black hair hiding his face, and kissed that same spot. Hot breath warmed her skin and added a sweet savor to the robe's teasing.

Savannah twined her fingers through his silken locks, urging him on. Beneath her fingers, she felt him tremble. Desire – fierce, tidal – raged within him. And yet, he roused her with slow, deliberate leisure. As if he feared the passions that were devouring him.

Brushing the robe aside, his mouth found her nipple and closed around it. Sucking, kissing. She moaned and shivered, arching her back to offer herself to his teasing mouth.

That sound, that soft cry of need, whetted his own desires. His kisses grew fiercer, circling her nipples, sliding across the skin of her breasts. A hand slipped beneath her robe and stroked the other globe, thumb circling, arousing the nub of her nipple.

With a sigh, she slid her legs apart, and he accepted that invitation, slipping between her thighs. The robe now hid nothing. Silken shirt and pants rubbed against her. The stark contrast – bare skin teased by his fully clothed body – added a delicious spice to his kisses. Vulnerable yet trusting, she was his.

Under the loving assaults of his mouth and hands, her breasts ached with a yearning, a need that sharpened as he abandoned them. Lower he moved, kissing a path across her stomach. His hands slid beneath her. Raising her, cupping her buttocks, stroking them. The silk-wrapped weight of his body slid lower too, gliding across her sex with a languorous stroke that set her panting.

Now, his mouth played across her belly, dipping low to brush against the fuzz above her sex. Fingers teased thighs and buttocks and stole furtive touches of what lay between. 'Assaulted' from both sides, her sex grew slick and wet, eager for its own conquest.

A whimper of sheer delight escaped her. Her body slipped free from her control. It twisted, wracked by her need, by her longing. Her hips bucked, pressing urgently against his chest. Begging him to finish this.

Todd was a distant, sad memory. A man whose pleasures peaked before hers even began. Jordan Beaumont was woven of a different cloth. Tossed by desire, she writhed beneath him, and only his ragged breathing betrayed the passion that burned within him too. She was his delight, his world. Pleasure was his gift to her, and the heat of her body set him on fire.

There was a pause, a tantalizing moment of stillness, then his mouth slid between her legs. Savannah cried out as those lips pressed a kiss against her most secret place. Her fingers curled the sheet, clawing at its soft cotton folds as desire took her.

Then, his tongue darted out. With hot, wet lashes, it whipped the eager nub of her sex. Sharp animal cries of pleasure were wrenched from her as his mouth pressed close. Hungry, devouring.

Too much, too great! Her passion rose, cresting like a wave that threatened to smash her against the shore. "Jordan! I can't... I can't..."

The same swell of desire seized him, shattering the last shred of his mastery. With a soft moan, he rose, rocking back on his heels. Hands that had caressed her so gently seized his shirt and ripped it open. With no thought, he cast it aside and scrambled to his feet, kicking off shoes and pants.

At last, he stood above her, freed from the prison of his clothes. His cock, hard and proud, jutted up. The moonlight that filtered in from the balcony transformed him. Sketched in shadow and moonlight, he seemed more statue than man. A picture of masculine perfection, like some old Greek god.

Only for a moment did he hold that pose before desire's tidal pull brought them back together. With the last shreds of his control, he lowered himself gently between her legs.

That was all he could manage. Her welcome, open thighs proved a lure he could not resist and with a soft cry, he drove into her.

Thick and hard, his cock slid in, filling her. Joined at last, their moans merged, woven together to form one song of animal need.

His hips worked, slipping his manhood in and out, between her hungry thighs. Each thrust stoked the blaze within her, and Savannah sobbed, consumed by a desire she had never imagined. Her cries urged Jordan on, driving his desire to a fever pitch.

Thought melted away, and there was only pleasure. A moment of pure ecstasy that caught her in its throes. She moaned, transfixed, consumed.

Once more, the ecstasy he brought her was his undoing. With a rush and a cry of release, he came in her, his seed spilling deep within.

All she could do was lay there, panting, caught in the vortex of that river of passion. Jordan withdrew and collapsed beside her. Strange though it was, she felt like a girl losing her virginity. The sex of her past was only a pale shadow of this bliss.

Savannah glanced over at the exhausted man by her side.

"Thank you. Thank you for showing me what love can be." She would never again be satisfied by the lukewarm 'pleasures' she'd known.

Black hair damp with sweat, Jordan smiled back at her. No sign of his usual cool demeanor; this was a man exhausted and fulfilled. "You are the oddest dream I have ever had," he whispered.

And then, the dream faded.

CHAPTER 4

*H*ow strange it felt to wake alone. To shower by herself, no male hands to caress the suds from her bare skin. To dress in private, with no one to mourn as the clothes stole her body from his view. Then to step out into the real world once more. Loud and noisy, full of traffic and crowds and meaningless bustle. The cold, sterile halls of Ormaz seemed more like a dream than last night's wonders.

A dull, hostile dream – full of jealous secretaries and leering executives. It was a relief to escape to the top floor and close the door of her office behind her.

Mr. Beaumont was already at work. Emerald eyes fixed on a computer screen, exactly where she'd left him last night. As the door clicked shut, he turned to her.

Some foolish corner of her heart searched his face eagerly, longing for a sign, a clue that something had changed. Some hint that the night of passion had been more than a dream.

Neither desire nor affection warmed those cold eyes. "Good morning, Miss Doucette."

"Good morning, master."

Disappointment welled within her – quickly followed by disgust.

Of course, nothing's changed, because nothing happened last night. I had a stupid dream about my boss.

Stupid… and hot.

And treacherous. I have a boyfriend, remember?

Yes, Todd. Todd, who never had time for her. Who always rushed through their trysts as if sex was a tedious chore. Who left her aching with unfulfilled need half the time.

Okay, so he's not perfect in bed.

Maybe 'not good' was more accurate.

So what? Todd is real – unlike my fantasy lover. Todd's real and he cares for me and he tries. I ought to be ashamed of myself for daydreaming about my boss like this.

"Miss Doucette? Is there something you wish to say?"

"What?" Oh, good heavens, she was still standing there. Lost in her thoughts like some ridiculous schoolgirl! "Uh, no, no master. I'm, uh…"

"Then I suggest you get to work. We have a lot to do." A touch of frost cooled his words, the lightest touch of a threat.

No Fang of Apophis tolerated a lazy minion.

And that's what I am, no matter what my dreams say.

It was a good reminder, one that helped dispel the last shreds of the night's delusions. Jordan Beaumont was, at best, a depraved and murderous Shifter. At worst, he was a Worm, one of the foulest creatures on the planet.

That's why I dreamed about that pile of bones.

And the tiny dragonfly.

The thought summoned its image to her mind. So fragile yet brimming with hope. The magical aura its wings spread through that dark realm.

Mr. Beaumont still watched her, his irritation growing more pointed. With a blush, Savannah hurried to her desk and buried herself in her work.

. . .

Hours passed in silence. When Savannah returned from lunch, she found him waiting for her. Her stomach knotted. Had she taken too long at lunch? Or... her mouth grew suddenly dry... had her master developed another 'hunger' he expected her to satisfy? One she would fight to avoid, even if it cost her life.

Unkind thoughts about Todd were bad enough. Betraying him was unthinkable.

There was nothing ominous in her master's demeanor, however. Hands folded in front of him, he kept his distance. His eyes didn't roam her body like it was some delicious treat he longed to devour. No, they remained fastened firmly – even decorously – on hers.

"Did you sleep well last night, Miss Doucette?"

Why would he ask that? "Um, yes?" she stammered.

At that waver, his eyes narrowed. "Truly? No dreams?"

Her heart leaped for one moment – and then dread dragged it to the ground.

Was it real? Some broken, warped version of the Rite of Claiming, the most sacred ritual of Dragons?

No, the logical half of her mind insisted that was impossible. Jordan Beaumont wasn't a Dragon and no other Shifters Claimed True Mates like them.

Do they? I mean, I've heard stories. People say that shared dreams are becoming a thing now that magic's returning to the world.

Rumors. Hearsay. She drove that thought away. If Jordan Beaumont had Claimed a Mate, he wouldn't let a full morning pass before he bothered to mention that fact!

And if your dream was right, then he's a Worm.

The idea of a Worm Claiming a Mate was too ludicrous for words.

Despite that dragonfly. Despite the hope it seemed to offer.

"Miss Doucette?"

"No. No dreams. I, um, usually don't remember them anyway."

What else could she say? The truth *had* to remain secret. If she told him she'd dreamt he took her, ravished her, brought her to heights of ecstasy she hadn't believed possible…

Why, that was practically a demand to be taken to the 'lounge' at once. Jordan Beaumont might be physically stunning, as gorgeous in real life as in her fantasies. But she did *not* want to sleep with him, no matter how attractive he was.

"Are you certain? Because you seem immensely distracted today."

There it was: the plain, ugly truth. Her master wasn't testing her, trying to subtly discover if they'd shared a dream. He was annoyed at her poor performance.

"I'm sorry. This promotion caught me flat-footed. It's, um, a lot to get used to. I'll do better tomorrow, I promise."

"See that you do." He scowled at the clock on the wall. "Mr. Adams wishes to discuss some nonsense with me. I fear my entire afternoon may be wasted – so, it's critical that at least *one* of us is productive. I've left a stack of scholarly articles on my desk. Follow up on them. I need to know how trustworthy they are."

"Yes, master." That pile was *tall.* To think that yesterday her worst fear was getting molested.

No time for that. I need to worry about being worked to death!

Head bowed, Savannah waited until he left before she slipped into his office. Few old journals were available online, which meant tomorrow would be spent trudging through the stacks of dusty libraries. As she scooped the papers up, she stole a quick look at Mr. Beaumont's computer screen.

It was on. And logged into Ormaz's network; logged into the private section, where minions like her were never permitted.

An email lay open. A polite welcome to the LA branch, mostly empty words. Except for the list of attached files.

Darkbornsurvey. Taossitecleanup. Hostages.

The air rushed out of her lungs in a gasp. Blackmail remained the strongest tool in the Fangs' arsenal. By taking families hostage they turned decent Shifters into reluctant traitors. If she could find out who was compromised, where their families were being kept…

To do that, all she needed to do was click on that link.

Riiiight.

It couldn't be that easy. Her new boss 'just happened' to walk off and leave her alone with critical information? No, this was a trap. An obvious test of her loyalty.

But the bait…

How many lives could she save?

Wasn't that worth the risk?

The best trap is one you can't resist stepping into, even after you see it.

If so, this was a fine trap. How could she pass up a chance to learn everything the Fangs knew about Nemagorix? Quickly, she locked the door to the office suite. It wouldn't stop security or slow down a dedicated attack, but it might buy her a moment if Mr. Beaumont returned unexpectedly.

She pulled a thumb drive out of her purse and sat down, heart hammering. Ormaz used a secure network; no emails left the building. Getting to the information wasn't enough. She needed to physically walk it out of the building.

She slid the cursor down to the first link. *Hostages.*

Nothing happened.

Click.

Savannah tensed, expecting the blare of alarms. Instead a new window opened, one that listed no less than six different prisons where hostages were held. Complete with names. With that information, other Shifters could figure out who was compromised.

I just found the key to learning which Rats are double agents!

Still, no warnings blared. No guards with assault rifles kicked in the door.

She dragged the file onto her thumb drive and selected another.

Click.

A report on an excavation near Taos that was compromised by the Darkborn. A danger she'd never even heard of.

Click. Drag.

Breath shallow and fast, she got to work. Sorting through Beaumont's email. Copying every file she could. Waiting for the trap to spring.

Which it never did.

Two hours and three thumb drives later, she had to quit. It was too dangerous. If Mr. Beaumont saw her in his office, she was dead. Or, worse, liable to be dragged off and tortured.

Despite her fear, though, her heart sang. This was the motherlode, the fountain of information she'd always dreamed of. *This* was why she'd spent three years undercover among the Fangs. Living for the day when she'd worm her way into their trust.

Living for today.

She needed to talk to Todd as soon as possible. Her survey of Ormaz's files made one thing clear: The Fangs of Apophis knew *a lot* about the Shifters of the Southwest.

Where the Aegis was and what protection it had. Which men were attuned to it. Who their loved ones were, where they lived. They even had full transcripts of some of the private meetings between the leaders of the different Kinds.

Which could mean only one thing: There was a Fang spy among the local Shifters. Someone highly placed. Someone trusted by both Dragons and the Witch Hares of Sedona, the most powerful Warren in this area.

Who that was, she couldn't tell. But maybe one of the other files held a clue to the spy's identity. With more time, Todd and the others might find him.

If she could get this information to him. She wasn't out of the woods yet...

Taking a seat at her own desk, Savannah scattered papers around herself. Building the perfect picture of hard work. For half an hour after that, she scribbled down meaningless notes.

Until Jordan Beaumont strode back into the office. Once more, she was struck by his aura. Even walking, he commanded respect. His poise, the strength and confidence of his stride... they were like nothing she'd ever seen in another man. Now, irritation layered a hint of danger on top of that.

The meeting had *not* gone well.

Good. It helped hide her guilt. Anyone would shrink away from that annoyance. Her dry lips and rapid heartbeat wouldn't betray her.

"Welcome back, Master."

"Eddy Adams is an idiot," was all he said.

One last test. As Mr. Beaumont returned to his computer, Savannah watched him from the corner of her eye. Was everything back where it belonged? Opened mail re-marked as 'unread'? Each window in its proper place? One slip, and she was dead. He might not even bother to call for security. Just snap her neck and be done with it.

Disgust twisted his handsome features as he surveyed the screen. Then, with a deep sigh, he went back to work.

Slowly, her heartbeat returned to normal. Head bowed, hands folded in front of her, Savannah crept to his door. "Master?"

"Yes?" He never even looked her way.

"As you feared, many of the papers I need are not online. May I have your permission to leave now? I want to spend some hours in UCLA's library."

Now, he *did* raise his head, fixing her with those uncanny, brilliant eyes. They held her, like a rabbit in a snare, and she feared that she'd overstepped. Instead, he merely said, "It's already late. Don't work all night just to 'impress' me. I want you rested and at your best when you're here."

Freakishly kind, for a Fang! "As you wish. But I can still get a lot done this evening."

"Very well."

Quietly, she backed away. Then, scooping up her pocket-book (and the precious thumb drives it contained), she hurried out the door. At every step, she expected security to come swarming out.

No one did. She rode down the elevator alone and swept past the checkpoint without raising an eyebrow.

Not until she reached the street did euphoria sweep over her.

I did it! I scored an incredible breakthrough against the Fangs!

Todd would be so happy! And the other Shifters too, of course. But it was the thought of her boyfriend's glee that set her alight.

CHAPTER 5

From his desk, Jordan could see Savannah 'Doucette' at every moment. Each time he glanced up from his computer, she was there. Long, luxurious, brown hair framing her heart-shaped face. Sweet, full lips pursed in concentration. Most Fang women reveled in edgy fashions. Purple hair, pancake make up, garish lipstick and eye liner. Not his secretary. She was a breath of fresh air in this decadent place. Clean and pure, only the lightest touch of rouge and color to accent her natural beauty.

Her soft, feminine form roused fierce emotions within him. Lust and longing, a sharp, possessive desire that made him want to attack any man that dared to cast an amorous look her way. She was *his.* His secretary. His assistant. For his eyes only. And he could watch her all day long.

I could do more. If I wished.

As her master, he could demand anything from her. His peers often did. Hell, his office even came equipped with a spare bedroom. The 'lounge' as they called it. People expected a Fang to bed his assistant – whether she welcomed his attentions or not.

The mere thought made him queasy, killing the desire that smoldered within him. He could never take her against her will. Oh, sure, he'd dreamed about her in a vivid (if pathetic) parody of the Rite of Claiming. As if a wretch like him could actually win a True Mate! Sad, really, that he still dreamed there was something pure inside him. Something a loving woman could see and desire.

In real life, though, Savannah 'Doucette' did *not* love him – nor desire him. Her body language screamed that, in the way she folded her arms across her breast as they talked, hiding them from him. The stoop of her shoulders, as if she sought to fold in on herself and avoid his gaze entirely.

That was not the posture of a smitten woman. If she wanted him, she wouldn't hide her body. She's flaunt it, find excuses to brush against him and be near.

None of that happened. They remained at opposite ends of their offices, two cool professionals.

Savannah 'Doucette.' Not for the first time, he found himself wondering what her real name was. Jordan's Rat detective was good – good enough to warn him that she was a spy. Not good enough, however, to uncover her true name.

Maybe that wasn't fair. Perhaps the 'problem' was that she was too competent. Yesterday, she snapped up all the information he'd left her. She must have; she wouldn't have fled the office so quickly if she was empty-handed. Yet, try as he might, he couldn't see any sign that she'd accessed his computer. That relieved him more than he cared to admit.

She may actually survive this. Unlike me.

How long had she hesitated, sure his 'carelessness' was a trick? He'd dragged the meeting out as long as he dared, until Eddy Adams squirmed with impatience, buying her as much time as possible. A cautious spy wouldn't leap at such a painfully obvious 'lapse.' Wariness kept them alive. He could only hope that his bait was too tempting to refuse.

Because it wasn't a trap. It was a gift.

With her help, I am going to destroy the Fangs of Apophis. Or at least its American branch.

Savannah rose. When she saw that he studied her, a blush brightened her cheeks. So alluring, so enticing, that his desire came rushing back full force.

"Master? May I take my lunch now?"

"Yes." He continued studying her. Courtesy was a weakness among the Fangs. A lapse that might warn them that he'd changed. So, he watched her, savoring the curve of her hips, the way she swayed gently as she left. Leaving him alone, with his work.

Time to find more information for my spy to 'steal.'

That should have been it. Once her distracting beauty vanished from his sight, his calm should return. Longing and desire would be put back to sleep by the tedium of dull work. For a few minutes, at least, all went as he planned.

Then it hit him. An explosion of fear that tore the breath from his throat and left him gasping.

Savannah was in danger. Mortal danger.

Trembling, Jordan leaned back in his chair. What a ridiculous idea. Ormaz wasn't without its dangers; no lair of the Fangs was. But he had no reason to believe his secretary was threatened. Even if she was, how on Earth would he know?

Something stirred in the dark recesses of his mind. Feelings, a voice that died decades ago.

...mate... it whispered.

His lip curled with scorn. As if a monster like him could Claim a Mate? Apparently, that dream had unleashed a torrent of foolishness. Triggered a... what was this? A panic attack? He'd never had such a fit of vapors before. Fear was as alien to him as love.

There is nothing wrong with Savannah. Stop this nonsense at once!

Instead, his horror doubled. Blood pounded in his temples, adrenaline roared through his body, demanding action. *Find her! Protect her! Save her!* No rational thought could blunt the edge of that command. His heart, his soul, *needed* to go to her, now. To his shock, Jordan found himself losing control. Rising to his feet, heading for the office door, even while he raged at himself for being a fool.

Movement shattered the last of his self-control. Like a river when it finally breaks free from its dam, his heart spurred him on. Two steps, three… and then, he was running. Throwing the door open, barreling down the hall, whipping past glass doors where secretaries stared at him in shock.

Not once did he question his destination. Savannah was in the lunchroom. Not at the cafeteria. Not gone out for lunch. How he knew this didn't matter. It was a fact. A certainty that drove him at top speed.

He hit the door at a full run. Already, his Shifter power flowed into him, preparing to do battle with whatever threat menaced his secretary. With a shriek of tearing metal, the door burst off its hinges.

A woman's scream joined the door's howl.

Savannah.

She sat, a homemade sandwich in her hands, staring in shock. Not at Lara Pearl, the only other person in the room.

At him.

Drowning in rage and the need to protect her, he barely noticed. The rational part of his mind protested that, of course, he'd frightened her. He'd just kicked the door in, hadn't he?

"Master? What's wrong?"

Empty noises spilling from her lips. What mattered was the threat. The enemy that dared to menace her.

Lara Pearl.

With a flip of his wrist, Jordan sent the table flying. It crashed against the wall, spraying shards of glass across the floor.

Again, Savannah screamed as she scrambled away from him, a sane, sensible act when faced with a raging Shifter.

Lara Pearl, however, simply stared at him. Facing his fury, his power, with shocking calm. "How interesting," was all she said.

Doors opened down the corridor. Shouts rang out, more meaningless noise. Nothing would distract him from his goal, however. "SAVANNAH, GET OUT!" he roared.

To his relief, she trusted him. With no hesitation, she darted to the doorway.

At once, he stepped between her and Pearl. His heart sang, a beautiful song – one he'd forgotten in the long, dark years. The rightness, the truth of protecting her, filled him with joy.

"How did you know?" Pearl asked.

Know what? Now that Savannah was safe, the rage that had driven him began to fade. Leaving a deep confusion in its wake.

What the hell is going on here? What did I just walk into the middle of?

More important, what on Earth was he going to do? As a lord of the Fangs, he could kill any secretary like her with impunity. No one would blink an eye – he could slay her simply because he disliked her tone. Adams might sulk over losing his secretary, but he'd get another. The Fangs were full of women like her.

But Jordan couldn't just kill her. Not without cause.

A harsh, croaking voice spoke in his mind. Feeble yet stronger than it was five minutes ago.

This... thing threatened... Mate.

Was that truly his Shifter soul speaking again, after so many years? The thought filled him with more dread than joy. Why was it babbling again about Mates? He couldn't...

Lara Pearl reached for him, as if she meant to give him a comforting pat on the arm.

Instinct made Jordan jerk away from her touch. As he did, the last clue fell into place.

Darkborn. Pearl wasn't in control of her body. Some malign spirit, some demon, wore her.

Something that thought *he* would be a much better host.

He spun away from her hand and caught one of the chairs. With a quick, savage blow, he slammed it into the secretary's leg. The bone snapped, sickeningly loud, and she dropped to the ground.

Silent, without any sign of pain. Which confirmed that the thing he faced was no longer fully human.

Behind him, Savannah gasped.

"Darkborn!" he shouted, never taking his eyes from his fallen foe. "Get a Witch Hare, now!"

Savannah tore off down the hall. She dodged Eddy Adams who sidled cautiously toward Jordan.

"Beaumont? What the hell is going on?"

"Darkborn. One got your secretary."

The creature tried to force Lara to crawl closer. Both Shifters backed away, and the spirit hissed with annoyance.

"Once the Witch Hare gets here, we'll get her dispossessed," Jordan assured the other lord.

A spasm wracked Lara's body. Her jaws wrenched open – and suddenly, a stream of black vomit spilled forth, pooling on the ground before her.

The Darkborn. Leaving her crippled form as it sought a healthy host.

Gasping, eyes wide with terror, Lara looked up at him. "Help me…," she whimpered. Then, the pain of her shattered leg hit her, and she wailed in agony.

Freed from her, the demon slithered eagerly toward the two Shifters. Jordan shifted his weight onto his toes, ready to dodge. If he could keep this thing focused on him for just a few minutes, long enough for Savannah to fetch the Hare…

Beside him, a gun shot rang out. Lara Pearl's screams were cut short as a bullet slammed into her head. And, like a shadow dispelled by the sunrise, the Darkborn faded away.

Shocked, Jordan spun.

Adams. A faint curl of smoke drifted from the barrel of his .45.

"Why the hell did you do that?" Jordan gasped. This woman was his *lover*! How could he kill her in cold blood?

His horror baffled the other Fang. "Didn't you read the report on these things? Darkborn stay anchored to their host, even when they emerge from its body. Kill the host and the demon goes back to the Other Side. Quickest way to get rid of them."

"But Savannah was getting a Witch. We could have saved her…"

Adams' nose wrinkled. "Lot of work for a secretary. Why bother? I can just get another one."

Without thought, without warning, Jordan's fist lashed out. It slammed into the bridge of Adams' nose, shattering it in a spray of blood, and knocking the Wolf into the wall. Howling, he crumbled to the floor.

Jordan kicked his feet out of the way and stalked down the hall. A deep, cleansing fury burned within him.

Savannah stood beside the elevator. Things had happened

far too fast for her to summon help. Seeing his rage, she shrank away.

"Come!" he snapped as he strode toward his office.

His office. *His* lair. A place for him and *his* secretary – and God help anyone who assaulted them in *his* domain!

No spiritual 'voice' spoke. Hell, he'd probably imagined it. Yet, a deep sense of rightness settled over him as he shut the door behind them.

This was what he should do.

This was what he should have done long ago.

*N*othing made sense.

Savannah stared out through the suite's bullet-proof glass walls as people scurried by. Many stole long, furtive glances as they did. Curious about the attack, and Mr. Beaumont's odd behavior.

Well, if they saw any answers in here, they were one up on her!

Her master had spent the last hour, pacing furiously, in his office. An agitation broken only by the occasional angry phone call. He seemed genuinely upset that Eddy Adams had killed Lara.

That was the first thing she simply couldn't understand. Why did he care? She did. Lara was sort of nasty – but she'd tried to help 'the new girl' in her own obnoxious, cutting way. That was kinder treatment than any new Fang could expect. Savannah was grateful for her snooty advice on clothes and how to please a master, even if she didn't intend to follow any of it. Her stomach roiled every time she thought of Lara's death. To watch the woman murdered... by her lover, no less! Because he couldn't be bothered to wait for a Hare…

Any normal person would be appalled. But Jordan Beaumont wasn't normal. He was a high-ranking Fang of Apophis. A monster. Probably a murderer many times over. His compassion baffled her.

Even it wasn't the question that truly frightened her. The one that shook her beliefs to the core was, how had he known?

Darkborn were notoriously subtle. Once they were hidden inside a host, not even a trained Witch Hare could detect them. Rumor had it that a psychic attached to the Sedona Warren could sense Darkborn. If so, that lady was unique. Those spirits were the ultimate spies and assassins. The almost-unstoppable hands of Nemagorix.

So, how had Jordan known Lara was possessed? What need drove him to kick down the door? It made no sense.

Irrational though it was, she wondered if she was to 'blame'.

Was I in danger? Did that spirit plan to possess me?

Nonsense. Only True Mates knew when their loved one was in danger. Despite her odd dream, Jordan Beaumont couldn't be her Mate. He wasn't a Dragon. He hadn't joined her in that strange, vibrant fantasy.

An image came to her, of the tiny, brilliant dragonfly. Savannah brushed it from her mind.

Strange as it was, that was nothing like the Rite of Claiming. If we truly were Mates, something would have changed.

And it hadn't. End of question. Silly, romantic fantacies would get her killed if she weren't careful.

Mr. Beaumont must have gotten an email about the traitor and decided to take care of it at once, before the Darkborn possessed someone else and they lost track of it.

That made a lot more sense than some silly notion of

Mates and true love.

The phone rang again. Mr. Beaumont's direct line. Savannah watched the button on her phone light up. Inside his soundproof office, her master paced and swore. When he slammed the phone down and stormed out, he was in a temper that made her quail.

"Meetings," he snarled.

No surprise there. He'd probably broken Eddy Adams' nose. No doubt, the other lords of the Fangs wanted an explanation. The Wolf was, at least in name, in charge of Ormaz Corp.

In the doorway, he paused. "Lock this door once I'm gone. Don't let anyone else in. If they insist, tell them it's on my orders."

No minion would dare disobey her master's commands. He'd given her a perfect excuse. Meekly, Savannah did as he said.

Then, alone and behind locked doors, she took stock of her options.

The safest course was 'do nothing.' Lara's death had kicked the beehive. And yet…

Chaos was the best cover. With Eddy injured, and the staff terrified, no one would pay any mind to her.

And there was more. In his agitation, her master had left his personal laptop behind. She could see it sitting open on his desk.

Anything he doesn't want other Fangs to see will be there.

Fangs were traitors at heart, treacherous and devious to the core. None of their senior members were trustworthy. Everyone plotted against his peers.

What secrets would that computer hold? What weapons that the Shifters of the Aegis could use against their enemies? It might even reveal the name of the Fang spy who had infiltrated their ranks.

In the end, she couldn't hold back. The temptation was too great. Coolly and efficiently – like her boss had ordered her to do this – Savannah fetched the computer. Then, she retreated into the 'lounge', the one room with solid walls no one could see through. Finally, the foul room served a good purpose!

Sure enough, Mr. Beaumont had left himself logged in. Giddy with excitement, she began to page through his secrets.

The first ones were... disappointing. Jordan Beaumont kept copies of all the research she'd done for him. He had a few extra analyses and spreadsheets crunching that data. Nothing that looked terribly important. None held any clues about the identity of the Fang spy. Savannah began to think she was wasting her time...

Until she checked his email.

No new messages – but as she scanned the list of read emails, one address leaped out at her.

griffin@swnet.com

Griffin Davis? The Chimera who'd been claimed by the Aegis? Why was he writing to a Fang of Apophis?!? Horror flooded through her at the thought. Did they truly have a traitor in their midst? One tied to the Aegis, no less? A man who had access to their most secret plots and discussions?

And there was worse. A few lines down, she saw another familiar address.

ghost@freedumb.com

No way anyone would forget that domain name! Ghost was a hacker with the Sand Pack, the strongest band of Wolves in this area. How many times had the woman uncovered some inexplicable clue online, some 'hidden' bit of information that saved the day for the Shifters of the Aegis?

Was she another traitor? Did her 'tips' come from the Fangs of Apophis?

Mind reeling, Savannah clicked on the first message, the one from Griffin. As she did, she finally spotted Jordan's own email address.

The mystery was solved.

nemo@hotmail.com

Nemo. A mysterious 'informant' who frequently sent hints to the Shifters of the Aegis. A person who seemed to know an awful lot about the Fangs of Apophis.

No wonder. Jordan Beaumont *was* Nemo. One of the highest-ranking Fangs of Apophis was helping the Shifters of the Aegis.

Or was he? Savannah tapped her pen against her lips.

Nemo certainly *seemed* to be one of the Good Guys. He'd revealed Fang plans to them, and even helped them find the Aegis when it got stolen. Why would a villain do that?

Maybe because he hates Nemagorix more than us. After all, the Fangs can't conquer the world if that thing destroys it first. The Aegis chose decent Shifters, not Fangs. If stopping the demon lord is Jordan's top priority, betraying the Fangs is a small price to pay.

That was the simplest explanation. The only one that made sense. Yet, another, more outlandish idea charmed her.

Maybe he wanted to switch sides. To redeem himself for all the wrongs he'd committed.

Once more, she remembered that dragonfly, the gossamer sheen of its wings, bright in the desolation. She recalled Jordan's politeness and restraint, so unusual in the Fangs. How Lara's murder had enraged him.

Could he be saved? Had he changed?

Again, foolish whims threatened to drag her down.

I don't know why he's 'helping' us – and it's not my place to figure that out. All I need to do is pass this information on to Todd.

Her boyfriend would know what to do.

The Shifters of the Aegis needed to know who Nemo really was.

CHAPTER 7

Todd was ecstatic.

They met at a ratty 'hotel' that rented rooms by the hour. Savannah slipped past whores, johns, and drug addicts on her way upstairs. Even the joy of seeing Todd again couldn't quite shake the disgust this place raised in her. She'd hoped they might spend some time together. Undercover work was lonely; it had been ages since she'd fallen asleep in his arms. On her way over, she'd thought that there was nothing she wouldn't give to feel loved once more.

After seeing the room, she changed her mind. Stained sheets and a rumbled cover with a half dozen cigarette burns. Mold on the ceiling and the stench of stale smoke clung to everything. One whiff of this place killed her desire, dead.

Even Todd's excitement wasn't enough to make her amorous again.

"Nemo!" he crowed. "You did it, babe! You cracked our biggest mystery!"

"I thought 'our biggest mystery' was how to activate the Aegis and use it to bind Nemagorix." The carpet *crunched* under her shoes. Savannah didn't even want to know why it did that.

"Well, sure. But this is *huge.*"

It was. And surely, something as important, as game-changing as this, deserved a reward? A hug? A kiss? A better hotel room where 'something' might happen?

That seemed to be the farthest thing from Todd's mind. "You need to get back into his personal accounts. Find out who he's contacted and what information he's shared with them."

"Why? Can't you just ask Griffin, Ghost, and the others? I'm sure they'd tell you."

"These are people who cooperated with a senior Fang," he sniffed.

"They didn't know that. Until now, *no one* knew who Nemo was."

"That's not a safe assumption."

"Todd," she sighed, "none of those letters gave any indication of treachery. Ghost and Griffin? We have *no* reason to doubt them. Just ask."

"How about you just do your job?" he countered. A sharp rebuttal that stung. Savannah felt the last traces of her joy fade away.

"I *am* doing my job." When her handler got in moods like this, it was hard to avoid rising to his insults. "However, it was a freak accident that gave me access to Beaumont's private computer. I doubt I'll be that lucky again."

"Make your own luck."

That was *so* not helpful. "It will be extremely dangerous."

She winced as he gave a harsh bark of laughter. "If you want a safe job, you should be flipping burgers at McDonald's."

"I just think–"

"No one pays you to think." His words hit her like a slap

to the face. "That's *my* job. I'm your handler, remember? I give the assignments. You carry them out."

He thought her an idiot? A mindless drudge following some man's orders? Did he have any idea what it was like to work undercover? The constant wariness it required, the ability to lie and improvise at a moment's notice? Not to mention the acting! One slip, one 'out of character' reaction, and she was dead. How *dare* he call her 'stupid'?

Even as her temper stirred, though, doubts assailed her. What did she expect? He was a Shifter, she mere Kin. Of course, he was in charge. No one in the First Flight or Shifters of the Aegis confided in her. Why, she ought to be grateful that she was any use at all!

In the end, all she said was, "I'll do what I can."

"Good." Without even a peck on the cheek, he headed for the door. "Can't wait to see your next report."

"Wait." He paused, frowning. "Todd, there are two other matters I want to discuss."

"Well, make it quick. We've been here too long already."

"What do you think about approaching Beaumont directly? His correspondence and behavior suggest he may be looking for a way out of the Fangs."

"I think that's an idiotic idea."

Ouch. Well, at least he made his feelings clear... "If we could turn someone in the Fangs, a senior member like Beaumont–"

"Do you have any hard evidence that he wants to leave the Fangs?"

She thought of that dragonfly. "No, but..."

"Then spare me your 'woman's intuitions'," he sneered. "Jordan Beaumont is a murderous, devious, back-stabbing monster. He's not going to change sides."

Todd hadn't seen Jordan's face when Lara was murdered, or the rage he turned on her killer. "But if he did–"

"No. It's too dangerous."

Now he cared about the risks she took? She could argue… but it seemed Todd was in a 'mood' tonight. Contrary and dismissive. No sense butting heads with him. She could make her own decisions without his permission!

"I'm not sure it's worse than the other dangers I face. Though that does bring me to my last concern. I think I should quit."

"What?" he yelped. Finally, *finally,* he stopped edging toward the door like he couldn't get away from her fast enough. "What are you talking about?"

"I don't think I should go back to work. Things are getting too hot."

"Don't be stupid! You can't quit now – not when you're on the verge of uncovering critical information!"

"I'm not learning anything useful about the Aegis or Nemagorix," she reminded him gently.

"So what? You learned Nemo's identity! You can't stop now."

"Todd, they just uncovered a Darkborn in the secretarial pool. The level of scrutiny I'm going to face will go through the roof. I've managed to break into their secure network twice, but a third attempt is too risky. Especially, right now."

"Risk is your job."

No love, no feeling, softened that order. Had any man ever sent his lover into danger so callously?

I bet Eddy Adams treated Lara that way.

It was an ugly, unkind comparison. But one her heart embraced.

In the midst of this argument, a picture drifted into her mind. Jordan Beaumont – stepping between her and Lara. Placing himself in the face of danger, to shield her.

Her. His secretary. An expendable, worthless minion.

He had guarded her. She knew that, trusted her feelings.

He had protected her and grieved that he couldn't save Lara as well.

That wasn't the way a loyal Fang behaved.

Heck, it was better treatment than her 'boyfriend' gave her! Todd still waited, tapping his foot with impatience. This was the point where she was supposed to cave, like she always did. Duck her head. Accept her assignment. Run whatever risk he sent her into.

Instead, her eyes narrowed. "Do you even care about me?" she hissed. "At all?"

Surprise widened his eyes – not pain. "Savannah, what...?"

She turned away, eyes burning. Words like hers would stab a lover through the heart. Yet, Todd was merely startled, as if she'd made an unexpected move in chess – not accused him of being unfaithful.

At once, he hurried to her and slipped his arms around her. Pulling her into an embrace she once loved. "Of course, I love you! You know that."

How many times had he said that? Hundreds over the last three years.

How many times did he show that in his actions?

Not one example came to mind.

"Babe, of course, I love you. And I'm proud of you. You've done so much..."

This time, she refused to surrender to his caresses, like she always did.

Lips brushed her hair aside and nuzzled at the base of her neck. Their touch made her skin crawl, and Savannah wiggled free of him. "You're right. We've been here too long. I should get going."

"Look, I know this is stressful."

Stressful? Watching a woman she knew get murdered was 'stressful'? That was an understatement!

"But you've made incredible breakthroughs! We just need to stick it out another year or so."

We. As if he shared the dangers and fears that she did! She ignored his fake concern and blandishments. "Next meeting in two weeks, yes? At the library?"

"Savannah, wait. Please."

In the doorway, she paused. They had shared too much, loved too much, for her to walk out after such a plea.

Brown eyes wide with contrition, he lowered his voice. Like a man trying not to frighten a skittish colt. "I know this job is lonely and that takes such a toll on a woman. Let me help you. Let me make you feel alive again…"

Once more, she considered that bed, with its faded, stained cover. She inhaled the foul scent of stale smoke. And somewhere down the hall, an outraged streetwalker screeched at the john who'd cheated her.

"I'll pass, Todd. But thanks."

Then she turned her back on her lover and walked out.

The first drops of grief rained down upon her as she trotted along the creaking hall. Todd and she were over. They were co-workers, nothing more.

What did that leave her? Distant parents and too few friends. For three years, she'd devoted her whole life to this job.

Time to see it through, then. To the end.

Despite their argument, she'd do what Todd asked. Go back to work and uncover more secrets.

Or die trying.

CHAPTER 8

That night, Jordan dreamed. This dream, unfortunately, was nothing like the delirious night of passion he'd 'spent' with Savannah. No, these were the nocturnal visions that haunted him. Past crimes and failures. The people he'd turned his back on. The myriad of evils that arose from his laziness and selfishness. The past was an accusing finger, pointing at him. He rarely dreamed but when he did, he dreamed like this. An endless litany of his sins.

Lara Pearl threaded her way throughout it. Watching, lips pinched, as he failed to save his wife. Clucking with disapproval as he woke up from a drunken stupor to the news that his son had died while he wallowed in self-pity.

"You failed me too," she whispered, as he staggered from one vision to the next.

"You weren't mine to care for."

"Still, you failed. Again."

That, he couldn't argue against. It was his life, after all. Failure. He failed everyone.

Except Savannah. His secretary was there when he staggered into the office, late. Safe and sound.

And subdued. Her morning greeting lacked its usual cheer and she stared at her computer screen with dull disinterest. Several times that day, he found her gazing blankly into space.

What do you expect? She watched a friend get murdered yesterday. Don't be so quick to congratulate yourself on finally 'saving' someone. She was forced to watch that horror – because of you.

Something murmured a protest within him, something that might once have been a soul. The same silent yearning that urged him to take her by the hand and drag her out of this place. Call a taxi, rush to the airport, buy two tickets to anyplace that wasn't here.

If I truly want to save Savannah, that's how to do it.

But he didn't. He did nothing. That was his specialty, after all. And when the endless workday finally expired, they went their separate ways. Her, to some empty apartment. Him to his – and those terrible dreams.

Only to return the next morning to the same dull tedium.

He needed to do something. Jordan knew that. If he didn't, despair would claim him again. Then drink and drugs and the abyss. Yet the hopelessness of it all, the endless darkness, sapped his strength. He couldn't even imagine a path forward.

Except when he looked at her. Savannah, his sweet, innocent spy. Saving her had been his first decisive act in years. Decades, if he was honest. A threat to her had roused him. Woken the Shifter he used to be. Years of sloth had fallen from him, like rust from a waking robot, and for one moment, he became himself again. The Shifter he was in his youth. A man of passion and action.

Now, that man threatened to fade away once more. Dragged down in the swamp he'd made of his life.

Until he looked at her. Again. As he had all morning. Brown hair warmed by the morning sun. Pale and subdued, yet with a fierce strength. She was his pillar, his hope. With her help, he could pull himself back to his feet.

Oh really?

Jordan snorted at his own romantic delusions. No clean Kin woman would waste her time on a Fang.

Yet some ridiculous corner of his heart insisted he was wrong. Savannah would help him. Why?

…mate…

The voice in his mind startled him. Had his Shifter soul actually spoken?

"I thought you were dead," he told it. With the door closed, Savannah couldn't hear him.

If his soul had, it said nothing in return. But that longing to walk out with her and never return came back.

Silly. Stupid. About par for his spirit.

His phone rang, interrupting his self-loathing. "Beaumont."

"Mr. Beaumont, this is Mariset."

The personal assistant of Lord Alester, who was the closest thing to a supreme leader that the Fangs had. She was also one of the most talented magicians in their order, a formidable Hare in her own right.

Alarm dispelled the fog of his self-pity and brought the world into keen focus. Why were the top tier of the Fangs suddenly calling him?

"It's a pleasure to speak to you again, Lady Mariset. I enjoyed meeting you in Marseilles."

"I as well. I'm pleased to inform you that we shall soon enjoy each other's company again." Alarms sounded in his head as she said that, but the Hare's tone was smooth and calm. "I'm in LA now. There's a matter we need to discuss."

Personal visits? Even worse. "My time is at your disposal, of course."

"Excellent. I believe it will take me an hour to drive from the airport. LA traffic is abominable."

"I shall await your arrival, Lady. Is there anything I need to prepare?" *Other than an escape route*, he thought.

"No, nothing. All I need is your advice."

He hung up then and steepled his fingers. What was Mariset playing at? No, that was the wrong question. What was *Alester's* game? Powerful as she was, Mariset was her master's pawn.

Fate, it seemed, sought to drive him into motion.

What about Savannah? He loathed the thought that he might drag her into peril. Should he give her the day off? Get her away, someplace safe?

Reluctantly, he dismissed that idea. Mariset would expect service. Coffee, at the least, and probably other chores. If he dismissed his secretary, that would be odd. At that moment, he couldn't afford any red flags.

In all likelihood, he was being paranoid. If the Fangs knew of his treachery, they wouldn't send a lone Witch Hare to confront him. By trying to protect Savannah, he might well doom them both.

He did, however, warn her of their exalted guest and, like a good assistant, she prepared. Coffee, a selection of teas, and a plate of delicious appetizers from a nearby deli. When Mariset arrived, everything awaited her.

The Hare breezed into his office like a queen. A red mane of hair fell in waves around her shoulders. Eyes like chips of sapphire and jade scanned the room, weighing it – and her reception. Then she strode past his shy secretary, straight to him. Their preparations had passed muster… and were thus beneath her notice.

"Mr. Beaumont." She offered a pale, slender hand.

Jordan bowed and kissed it graciously. "Lady Mariset. Please, have a seat."

Only one man accompanied her, a short, skinny youngster with washed-out red hair. Shifters saw each other's souls, and a sick-looking Hare crouched by the man's feet.

Because of that, Jordan immediately dismissed him. Another Hare. Not a threat.

"How can I be of assistance?"

Mariset snapped her fingers. At once, the male Hare withdrew an object from his satchel. Something small and flat, wrapped in folds of silk. His mistress set it on Jordan's desk and pushed the edge of the cloth back to reveal a disk of yellowed wax. "Do you know what this is?"

There was something inscribed on it. A curving figure, covered in scales...

Jordan snapped back, glowering at the Witch with sudden suspicion. "It's a spirit trap. The pattern mesmerizes the viewer – even one as powerful as a Dragon. We dug it up in one of the Greek isles."

Were the Fangs onto him after all? Send two Hares in to lull him into complacency... and then spring a trap?

Mariset, however, shook her head. "Sadly, no. We lost that artifact. The damned First Flight captured it when they assaulted our bases on Criehaven. This," she pulled the disk out of its cover, "is what that thing inspired us to make."

The scaled figure was a worm biting its own tail. The Worm Ouroboros, devouring itself. A familiar image from early magic. To his relief, it didn't hold any special power. Nothing to fascinate or bind. He took the piece of wax from her and inspected it. "What does it do?"

"By itself? Nothing. It's just a focus. It reacts when it's in the presence of certain magics."

"So, it's a detector? Why bring it to me? Magic is your job." A hint of disapproval frosted his words. Lady Mariset might be the Fangs' foremost Witch Hare, but he was ancient and important too. She had best think carefully before she wasted his time.

Eyes glittering with vindictive pleasure, she leaned forward. "Because this changes everything. *This* is the future of our war against the First Flight and the Shifters who refuse to submit to us. At the moment, we only have a handful of Hares strong enough to use it. I, of course, am one. Master Alester sends me to you to demonstrate its power. Once you understand, you are to develop a plan to deploy it. To use it to destroy our enemies, once and for all. A great honor," she added with a faint sniff that suggested perhaps he wasn't worthy of such trust.

Indeed, he wasn't. Jordan was already planning how to get this information to Savannah. The First Flight needed to know about this new weapon.

First, though, he had to learn what it did. "An honor indeed. Show me its power, then."

"Of course."

Mariset began to hum, a tuneless sound that grated on his ears. Up and down, the note fell. To him, it seemed like random noise. For two minutes, she droned on endlessly, and Jordan found himself growing impatient.

"How long does this take?" he asked.

Or, he meant to ask.

No words passed his lips, however.

Startled, he tried again.

This time, his mouth wouldn't even open.

Too late, Jordan realized that his original fears were true. The Fangs *did* know that he was a traitor. They knew he was a Worm too, and that arrogance was the Achilles Heel of his Kind. Yes, they sent two Hares to bring him down. Enemies he would ignore in his pride. Threats he couldn't take seriously.

Until it was too late.

The waxen image of Ouroboros moved, twirling in a slow, stealthy circle that seemed to echo in his mind. His thoughts spun through rage, shock, and shame, touching each emotion, yet never staying with any long enough for it to break the lethargy that held him in place. Dimly, he could see Savannah, watching this scene through the glass of his office wall.

Run! he yearned to scream. *Save yourself!*

Not even his feelings for her could break the spell, though.

Mariset raised a long, thin finger, careful not to let the 'song' slip or fade.

"Mr. Beaumont?" her assistant asked. "Can you hear me?" When he did not answer, the junior Hare giggled. "It worked. It actually worked!"

With one flick of his wrist, Jordan could snap the wretched man's neck. What a pleasure it would be to wipe that triumphant sneer off his face!

If he could move.

The assistant scrambled to his feet and stepped out of the office; Jordan's heart froze. He was going to kill Savannah. If the Fangs knew about him, surely, she was in mortal danger too?

Instead, the Hare yanked open the suite door. "Mr. Adams? It's done."

Eddy Adams strolled in. With his broken nose and two black eyes, he looked more like a raccoon than a Wolf. But the elephant gun he held in his hands was no laughing matter. "So, you're that bastard Nemo who's been causing us so much trouble."

How the hell did they know that?

Adams raised the rifle to his shoulder. A move that made

Mariset's aide bite his lip. "Are you sure a mere gun will suffice?"

"Yeah. These days, they've got bullets that'll punch through steel. Good enough to splatter this traitor's brains all across that wall."

One last time, Jordan screamed at his body.

Move! Kill them! Save Savannah!

But the spell's iron bands bound him, completely. This was how they'd taken out Aaron Cole, that Dragon from the First Flight. Helpless, he stared up at the gloating Wolf.

"This is my lucky day. I can't tell you how long I've wanted to put a bullet in your arrogant face. Why…"

A shot rang out, shattering the stillness.

That weird, enchanting song ceased abruptly. Mariset's mouth opened in a tiny 'o' of surprise as a red stain blossomed on her chest. Then, she crumbled to the ground, blood pooling beneath her.

Adams and the aide spun, seeking their new enemy.

Behind her desk, Savannah stood. A .357 in her hand and grim determination on her face.

"You bitch!" Adams snarled. Once more, he snapped the rifle up and Savannah dropped to the ground behind her desk.

But his secretary was a smart woman. A brilliant woman. She'd broken the magical chains that bound him, and before Adams could squeeze off a shot, Jordan swatted the gun out of his hands.

Terror swept across the Wolf's face as he realized his enemy was free.

"Sorry, Eddy." Fangs appeared in Jordan's mouth as he smiled. "This *isn't* your lucky day."

CHAPTER 9

Savannah didn't have much to say as they fled LA. Once they were free of the city's traffic, Jordan's sleek BMW ate up the road. Within two hours, they arrived at a small rest stop. In the town of Beaumont, no less, a fact that amused her.

Distracted by their problems, her former boss didn't even notice. "This is where we part ways. You have a phone, yes?"

"Yes. Where will you go?" He had plans of his own, but she had one as well. One he *wasn't* going to like.

"Best if I don't tell you."

"I see."

He waited, expecting her to leave. Instead, she remained, planning the best way to make her pitch.

Jordan was the first to break the silence. "I do have one question for you. What's your name? Your real one."

With a jolt of surprise, she stiffened. "You know?"

"That you're a spy for the First Flight? Yes."

"How long...?"

"A month. It's why I picked you as my assistant."

"So you could feed me information. Like the other day,

when you 'accidentally' left yourself logged into the Fangs' secure network." He nodded. It made sense, though it deflated her pride a bit.

Guess I wasn't as clever as I thought.

She stole a glance at his face. Calm and stoic, no one would ever guess his life had just been ruined. "I'm surprised you're not angry with me. After all, this is my fault."

"No, it's not. I didn't feed you any information on my Nemo persona."

"You didn't need to," she confessed. "I found that out myself."

"Oh." No anger, no shock. Jordan simply wrinkled his nose. "I guess I had that coming. That's what I get for under-estimating you."

They both stared out at the traffic streaming by. A bruised, sore silence between them, until Jordan spoke once more.

"So, what is it? Your name. If you're willing to tell me, of course. I admit, I'll have a hard time not thinking of you as 'Savannah.'"

"You won't have to. That's really my name. The best lies are close to the truth – I didn't want to take some fake name like 'Alice' and then forget to answer when someone called me."

"Savannah…?"

"Savannah Dare."

A smile split his handsome face. Genuine, warm. Its touch dispelled the gloom that always surrounded him and added an impish gleam to his emerald eyes. For a moment, she saw Jordan Beaumont as he could be. Calm. Proud. Happy.

"That is an auspicious name. A strong name. One you live up to."

"Thank you."

"Thank *you* for saving my life. You didn't need to. No," he held up a hand as she began to protest. "No one tied you to my treachery. After they dragged my corpse away, you could have walked out a free woman."

"And give up the chance to assassinate the Fangs' greatest Witch Hare?" she scoffed. "Forget it."

"Ah, I see," he chuckled. "It had nothing to do with me at all, then?"

"Well, I wouldn't go that far." God, she could sit here with him all afternoon. Chatting. Getting to know each other. Away from the Fangs, it was so easy to forget what he truly was.

Self-indulgence like that wouldn't help either of them. The truth couldn't be denied and shouldn't be ignored.

Time to start the ugly, dirty part of this. Savannah took a deep breath and pulled out her phone. "Since you know what I am, there's no point making this call in private."

One ring. That's all it took before Todd answered. "Savannah? Where are you?"

Seriously? That was his first question?

"Are you okay?" he added quickly.

All right, that was a little better. But a hint of panic echoed in his words. A worry so deep it was suspicious. "I'm fine. What makes you think anything's wrong?"

"You're calling on the emergency line two days after we met. I *hope* to hell this is an emergency."

Oh, good point. Dammit, this work had made her paranoid. Here she was, doubting her own handler. Her *lover*.

Though, she wasn't crazy. Somewhere there *was* a rat. "Have you shared the information I gathered on Nemo?"

"Yes."

"With whom?"

"Uh, hell. With Finn Donnelly from the First Flight... the Sedona Warren... several of the Shifters of the Aegis... the leader of the local Rats... Why?"

Shit. No telling who the spy was, then. "Somebody told the Fangs. I barely made it out alive."

"Oh hell, babe, are you all right?"

That was better. That sounded like the Todd Manning she knew. "I'm fine, but my assignment is definitely over."

"Do you know what happened to Nemo? Er, Beaumont?"

"Yes."

He gave her a moment to volunteer more info. When she didn't, a note of petulance crept into his voice. "And...?"

"And I need to think about what I'm going to do."

"No," the Bear growled. "You need to tell me what you know and then *I'll* tell you what to do."

"Not this time, Todd." Annoyed herself, she hung up, quickly switching the phone to airplane mode, so he couldn't pester her.

Jordan pointed at the phone. "Your contact?"

"Yes. He passed my information on, so there's no telling who the traitor is."

"Do you trust him?"

"Yes."

Did that word tremble? Did she hesitate? Jordan kept watching her, a faint frown creasing his brow.

"Yes," she repeated. With more confidence this time.

"Good." He, unlike her boyfriend, didn't question her every move. "Is there someplace better that I can drop you off?"

Savannah turned toward him. Some conversations demanded you look the person in the eye. "No, but I'd like you to come to Sedona with me. Or, better yet, to Cortez, Colorado."

Cortez was a tiny town on the edge of Canyons of the Ancients National Monument. She wasn't sure he knew the place.

But he *did* know his 'enemies.' "That's where several of the

Shifters of the Aegis live. Are you suggesting I meet with them?"

"Yes. I'd like both of us to go."

Jordan's lip curled back into a sardonic smile. "Do I look suicidal?"

"I'm not suggesting you kill yourself. Just share your information with them."

"Then what?" His smile deepened into a sneer. "They'll just let me walk away?"

She met the scorn in his eyes. Chin raised, unflinching. "If I vouch for you… yes, I think they will."

"Savannah…" Like ice melting beneath a rush of hot water, his contempt crumbled. Not into acceptance, as she'd hoped. Into despair. "You don't understand."

"You've done terrible things. I know." Startled, he looked at her. "What those things are, I haven't a clue. But you're a senior member of the Fangs of Apophis. You don't get a position like that by being a nice guy."

"Oh, it's worse than that." Now, his chin rose in rebellion. "I'm a Worm."

A Fallen Dragon. One that had committed a form of spiritual suicide. She couldn't say she was surprised. Not when she recalled that dream, and the 'Dragon'-fly.

That was my subconscious letting me know it recognized his Kind.

Braced by that, she met his burning gaze without flinching. "I figured as much. Most Fang leaders *are* Worms."

"Then you know you *are* asking me to kill myself." Was it pain that roughened his voice and put an edge to his words? Did he feel betrayed that she cared so little for him?

"No, I'm–"

"Yes. If I go before those two Dragons, they'll kill me. They *might* listen to me first. Then again, they might not. Dragons hate us – with good reason. They kill us on sight."

"I'm willing to bet that no Worm ever asked a Dragon for help or protection. If you do…"

Jordan's head snapped back in revulsion. Perhaps the idea of begging for help stung his pride. Worms were once Dragons, after all, and nothing had an ego as large. "Why would I ask them for help?"

Had he not thought this through at all? Exasperated, she put a hand on his knee. At her touch, he flinched – but did not pull away. "Jordan Beaumont, what do you think happens next? What are you going to do?"

"I'm going to, uh, drop you off somewhere safe. Then leave. Find a bolt hole in some faraway place. Somewhere the Fangs can't find me."

"And what? Hide for the rest of your life? Alone? Looking over your shoulder every moment, worried about Fang assassins?"

That stung his pride. Jordan glared down his nose at her. "I am not such a coward as that. I will dispatch anyone they send against me."

"And then you'll have to flee. Again. Find another bolt hole. Hide. Wait for the next assassin. Over and over again, forever."

He laughed; a harsh, bitter croak that lacked all humor. "That's life."

"No, it isn't. Or, well, life doesn't *have* to be like that."

"I suppose it could also be extremely short and end beneath a Dragon's claws."

"True. Or you could join us. Take a stand against the Fangs. Help us defeat them. At least, then, you wouldn't be alone."

"Savannah…," he sighed. Once more, his habitual melancholy enveloped him.

"Listen to me." She squeezed his knee, a gesture that won her a bemused smile. "People deserve a second chance."

"Not Worms. You don't understand. My Shifter soul is dead. It killed itself."

That wasn't right, was it? "I thought Worms had Worm spirits. Sort of like insane, speechless Dragons."

"Most do, yes," he grumbled. "Mine simply died."

She didn't know what to think about that. Even more reason to drag him to meet other Shifters. People who knew so much more than a mere Kin woman. "Look, I'll vouch for you. I'll tell them how kind you were to me. How much it upset you when Lara was murdered. As Nemo, you've given us a lot of help. And... hey! Don't you know people who work with the Shifters of the Aegis? Ghost and Griffin?"

"Ghost, no. Griffin...," he grimaced, "yes, but I doubt he'll give me a good word. I've screwed him over several times."

Maybe – but the mention of Griffin gave her an idea. "If anyone understood the importance of second chances, it's Griffin. Did you ever think that Shifters would tolerate a Chimera?"

"No," he admitted. "Though, most Chimeras are murderers and cannibals. Griffin's pretty unique on that score."

"Like you're unique on the Worm-score."

"I'm hardly unusual."

"Didn't you just get done telling me that you don't have a typical Worm soul?" She didn't believe that it could truly be dead. She wouldn't have imagined him as a dragonfly if she did.

Yet, even her best logic couldn't sway him. Jordan shook his head. Years of darkness and despair had sapped his will, and reason wouldn't make him budge.

Well, reason wasn't the only weapon in her arsenal. Savannah scooped his hands up – and felt a flash of delight at the startled pleasure on his face when she touched him. "If you really want to leave, then look me in the eye and say it.

Tell me you don't mind being alone, forever. That you're happy living on the run and in exile. If you can look me in the eye and say that, I'll drop this."

"I…"

Flustered by her touch, by the warmth of her soft skin, he stared out at the traffic.

"That's what I thought. You *don't* want to 'live' like that. Deep in your heart, you know that's not life. It's existence."

He swallowed, still unable to face her, and she knew she'd won. All she needed was his consent. "Dare. Try to find a path out, a road to a better life. A *true* life. One with friends and comrades. I know there's good inside you. You've been trying to do good for years now. You just don't know how. But I do. Let me help you. Let *us* help you."

Surely, he would bend? The lure of friendship, of kindness, would tempt him?

"All right," he murmured. Words of surrender not hope. "I'll go with you. They'll probably kill me, but you're right: It's not like I'm really alive anyway. Why shouldn't I let a Dragon put me out of my misery?"

Not the reaction she'd hoped for.

But it would do. He'd agreed to come.

Now, it was up to her to save him.

CHAPTER 10

Things went about as badly as Jordan expected.

Their arrival at Sedona triggered a small panic. The first woman who spotted him immediately Shifted into a Hare. She stomped a quick warning, then spun around and charged directly into a wall in blind panic. Eventually, Danielle LePierre, the Queen of the Warren, emerged, pale faced. Despite Savannah's pleas, she sent them away to a park, where they were to await representatives of the Shifters.

Those turned out to be Dragons. Two of them. Kind of flattering that they feared him that much. Finn Donnelly, from the First Flight, was an old warrior, his spirit a hulking white Dragon whose scales bore the scars of many battles. A smaller black Dragon accompanied him, with the distinctive curled horns of the Flight of the Snows. Casey Briggs.

Living proof that two feuding Dragon Flights can get along when they face a common enemy.

Unfortunately, that 'enemy' was him.

Jordan's 'bodyguards' took him and Savannah to a house

on the edge of town. A bright, airy ranch with miles of scrub around it.

The Worm wasn't fooled. It was a prison, no matter how pretty it might be. They wouldn't allow him to leave until his fate had been decided. The four of them settled in and waited for his jurors, senior members of the local Shifter community, to arrive.

The sofa was plush and comfortable, the view over the desert was serene.

Jordan was content. This wasn't a bad place to die.

No, the person he pitied was Savannah. So hopeful. So foolishly optimistic. The Dragons' grim vigilance didn't dim her spirits at all. She chattered, she joked, she teased, fighting valiantly – and vainly – to take the chill from the room. Briggs joined her, half-heartedly. Donnelly paid her no more mind than a playful puppy. With fixed, unwavering attention, he watched Jordan, tense as a coiled spring. A fox hound, just waiting for its master's order to tear its prey apart.

When the time comes, he's the one who kills me. That other Dragon's a bit too civilized. Donnelly's a thug.

Probably a good thing. A person who spent a lifetime killing knew how to do it quickly and painlessly. Jordan didn't expect to be tortured and at least Donnelly would make sure he didn't suffer.

And so, they waited. Savannah fighting to make people comfortable, Jordan waiting to die.

Around dusk, the others arrived. The roar of motorcycles filled the air as three Wolf Packs arrived: Sand, Sage, and Big River. Only their Alphas came inside for the trial, though. The others took up outside and entertained themselves, racing and doing wheelies on their bikes.

None of the Wolves looked happy to be here. Aaron King, the Sand Pack's leader, scowled at the white Dragon. "This trial shit better not get to be a regular thing."

"We've only had two," Donnelly grumbled back.

"That's two too many."

Genuine irritation lit the big man's eyes. "There's no pleasing you, is there? If the First Flight decides on its own, we're tyrants. If we share the decision with you, you still piss and moan."

Most Shifters knew better than to annoy a Dragon. But King was an Alpha, and he didn't back down from anyone. "Sharing? What the hell do you think you've got to share with us? What gives you the right to decide a man's fate?"

"Power," Donnelly snapped. "We have the power to change things, so we are morally required to decide. Even choosing not to choose is a decision."

"So, choose already. Don't drag the rest of us into your squabbles."

"Our fight against the Fangs of Apophis isn't a squabble. It affects all of you, not just the First Flight."

Jordan leaned back, pursing his lips. *This* was why decent Shifters hadn't managed to wipe out the Fangs. Old feuds and new arguments constantly ripped the 'Shifter community' apart.

Briggs rose to his feet, hands joined in front of him, and bowed politely to the irate Wolf. His calm, level tone broke through the budding fight. "Aaron King, Alpha and father of my Mate. Hear my words, I ask you. As Wolves, you and the other Alphas are guardians of freedom. I understand why these trials grieve you, and I respect your honor.

"If you wish to take no part in these proceedings, you are free to go. I will inform the others of your choice." Donnelly opened his mouth to object, but the black Dragon raised a hand. "However, I remind you that this man, Jordan Beaumont, has harmed many. Perhaps, members of your own Packs. Do you not wish to hear his words and decide if he has wronged you?"

Not a word passed between the three Wolf Alphas – but they seemed to come to some silent agreement, an agreement that King voiced. "Well, when you put it that way... yes. But this shit has to stop. That's all I'm saying."

Donnelly rolled his eyes, earning another glare from the Wolves. Briggs, ever polite, bowed. "I hear your concerns and will honor them."

Yeah, he is definitely not the guy who's going to execute me.

Other judges straggled in. Danielle LePierre, Witch Queen of the Sedona Warren, breezed through the door and immediately took the seat at Donnelly's right hand. She offered the Dragons courteous greetings... and ignored the rowdy Wolves completely.

That's a lady who won't ask why she's here. She knows she's 'worthy' to decide a man's fate.

Finally a wizened old woman in Army fatigues slunk through the door, closely followed by a Bear in a polo shirt and jeans.

SueSue Mint, the elder of the local Rats. I've seen her picture. So that Bear must be Rex Fairburn, the guy who found the Aegis. First one bound to it.

In Fairburn, Savannah finally found an ally. He alone joined her in her small talk, radiating a calm, friendly cheer. Between them, they managed to dent the cold, funereal air of the room.

Now, all five Kinds were represented. Yet the door opened again to admit another face he knew from photos. Griffin Davis, Chimera. As 'Nemo', Jordan had worked with him, on and off, for years – though, they'd never met in person. Craggy and tall, the Chimera looked even more uneasy than the Wolves. Again, no surprise. That first trial King bitched about? That was Griffin's, to decide if the Shifters were willing to give a Chimera a chance to prove that not all of his Kind were monsters.

The two of them went way back… but it wasn't all good history. Griffin held himself aloof, away from Jordan. Cool and wary. "So. Nemo. We finally meet."

"Griffin." He waited for more, but the Chimera jammed his hands in his pants. "Trying to decide whether to punch me or shake my hand?"

"Basically. Yeah. Think I'll just take a seat." As he did, Griffin peered about the room. "Am I blind, or is Nemo's Shifter spirit hidden?"

"Jordan Beaumont is his real name," Donnelly said, "and no, it's not hidden. Apparently, it doesn't show up for some reason. He says it's dead."

Throughout all the introductions, Savannah had held her peace. Jordan understood. She was Kin, not Shifter. Fairburn was a friendly guy, but most Shifters didn't consider Kin their equals. Smart mortals learned to keep quiet around them.

Still, the woman carried herself with confidence and grace. She knew her worth, and he was pleased to see it.

She probably still thinks she's got a chance to save me, which is ridiculous.

The door opened one last time. Another Bear entered and, this time, his secretary cringed.

That gesture, subtle as it was, put Jordan on immediate alert. He tensed, eyeing the Bear, seeking the danger that Savannah sensed.

Or was he a threat? A second later, she rose and walked over to the newcomer. To Jordan's shock, the stranger pulled her into a fierce embrace and kissed her, passionately, on the lips.

Hot anger roared through him. Who was this man to touch her? *His* secretary! *His* woman! *His…*

…mate… a soft voice whispered in his mind.

Donnelly leaned forward, coiled menace ready to strike.

That movement tore a rift in the mist of protective fury that clouded Jordan's vision.

What the hell was wrong with the Dragon?

Then he felt it. The hint of power flowing through his body, an echo of his long dead Shifter soul.

When it stirs, my eyes glow with power. Almost like I was still a Dragon. Donnelly probably thinks I'm about to attack someone.

He forced himself to look away from Savannah. That must be Todd Manning, her handler. Her lover. A man who had every right to kiss her. Unlike him.

Jealousy stirred his dead soul once more, but he swallowed it. His eyes dimmed; the Dragons relaxed…

Until Manning broke the kiss and shook Savannah so hard it startled a squeak of pain from her. "Don't *ever* hang up on me again!"

That was too much. Rage bloomed within Jordan, sweeping away all thought of his own safety. He rose, ignoring the Dragons who leaped to their feet as well, and thundered, "Unhand her, or I will snap your neck."

Claws sprang from Donnelly's fingertips as his Dragon began to seize control. But before he Shifted, Briggs caught his arm. All eyes turned toward the startled Bear and the squirming woman he still held.

Quicker than anyone else, King spoke up. "Hey, asshole! Get off that woman! Now, or I beat the shit out of you."

Manning gaped at the Wolf but let go of Savannah's arms. She immediately took a step back, out of reach. "It's okay. She's my, uh, girlfriend."

"No, it's not okay." King stepped closer, forcing the Bear to retreat. "Can you not tell when a woman doesn't want you mauling her?"

The chivalrous gesture brought bitter bile to Jordan's throat.

I should be doing that. I am the one who ought to protect her.

Fairburn joined King, his pleasant smile fading away. "Not a good time for this, Manning. Why don't you step outside and let us get this done?"

"I'm Savannah's handler," he protested. "You'll need my testimony."

"Wait outside then," LePierre ordered. At her feet, her Hare glared at Manning, its teeth grinding softly. That was about as aggressive as Witch Hares got – a sign that the Bear's behavior angered her as well.

"Fine." He edged around the scowling Wolf but paused in the doorway. "Come on, Savannah. We need to talk."

"Not now." Arms folded across her chest, she backed away from him. "I need to be here."

Her loyalty to him made Jordan's heart sing.

The impact on Manning was the exact opposite. "Come, now!" he hissed.

That was the last straw. Once more, that power, almost forgotten, swept over him. Jordan rose, eyes blazing, and howled, "She is *not* your dog! You will not speak to her like one!"

Why did those words sound strange? Hissing, sibilant, like a threat from an angry serpent?

His teeth! With a shock, Jordan realized that his teeth had transformed into long, sharp fangs. Scales flashed down his arms, burying them beneath thick, protective armor.

I'm... Shifting? How...?

As soon as he noticed it, the changes stopped. In fact, the scales and teeth began to melt away, returning him to his human form.

Not before the other Shifters noticed, however. "Your 'dead' Worm is getting pretty rowdy," Donnelly said. Briggs kept quiet but he studied Jordan, lips pursed.

And Manning? He took the hint and fled as the three Wolf Alphas closed, ready to carry out their threat to beat him senseless. They chased the Bear out the door and paused, yelling insults after him until LePierre cleared her throat.

"May we get started? Please?"

Satisfied that they'd run Manning off, the Wolves returned to their seats. Savannah pulled her chair close to Jordan's side. Her presence, the shy, delighted glances she sent his way, quickly soothed his anger. Scales softened until he was fully human once more.

Then, the trial began.

And his secretary's smile disappeared.

Completely.

Hours passed. Jordan was honest; he'd committed a lot of sins. Strange, the pain of confessing far outweighed the pain of committing them. Perhaps it was because Savannah was there. Each admission, each statement of guilt, chipped away at her faith in him. He could see her wilt, slowly but steadily, as the minutes ticked away.

Yet she never despaired. When Donnelly summed up the account, long past sunset, Savannah was ready.

"So, robbery... fraud... embezzlement... blackmail..."

"Bad, but they hurt no one," she interrupted.

The Dragon gave her a cool stare. "Physically, no. Blackmail's nasty, though. Plus, Mr. Beaumont admits to a couple dozen killings... that he can remember. Probably more."

"None in cold blood, though." Trust her to see the good side of everything, no matter how small it was. "He isn't a murderer. He was a... a soldier. For a very bad cause."

Even Briggs sighed at her unflappable cheer. "Ms. Dare, it is clear that you wish this man pardoned."

"I do." She held her hand out to Griffin, who'd been very

quiet. "You got a second chance. Why not Jordan? Is a Worm so much worse than a Chimera?"

The Chimera shook his head. "The difference is, I hadn't actually done anything wrong. Beaumont has."

Tough to argue against, Jordan had to admit. But bless her if Savannah didn't try her damnedest. "He's also done good things. He's changed. He's working to put things right. Doesn't he deserve a chance to do that? To fix what he broke?"

Mutters and grumbling met her words, until, once more, Briggs' gentle bass quelled the noise. "Perhaps, then, you would best persuade this court by explaining. What has Jordan Beaumont done to convince you he still has good in his heart, despite the fact that he is a Worm?"

"Well, personally, I haven't known him long. But he was kind to me. The Fangs allow their executives, the 'masters', to abuse secretaries like me. Rape them, even, if that's what they want. Jordan was always a gentleman. When another secretary was possessed by a Darkborn spirit, he fought to save her. He would have succeeded too, if her master hadn't shot her. When he did, Jordan attacked him – even though he was the head of Ormaz Corp."

No one looked horribly impressed, and he couldn't blame them. Weighed against the people he'd killed, that was a small benefit.

"Anything else?"

Frustrated by their lack of support, she nodded. "For years, he's spied for us. How many Shifters have received tips and help from 'Nemo'?"

Now, she got her first help. Aaron King cleared his throat and nodded at Briggs. "He helped my daughter figure out who stole from the Flight of the Snows. Seems to me, you kinda owe him. Hell, we all do. Nemo told us where to find the Aegis when the Fangs stole it from Lucas Clay. Without him, we wouldn't have any tool against Nemagorix."

Before Savannah could push that further, Griffin shook his head. "I've dealt with him longer than any of you. If there's one thing I know about Nemo… er, Jordan here, it's that he has his own reasons for doing things. Don't assume his 'gifts' are meant to help you."

The closest thing to a friend he had, and the man wouldn't speak up for him.

That is a sad commentary on the state of my life. Even worse? I can't say he's wrong.

Savannah could though. "Bullshit. Look at the information he just shared with us. How is that not a gift? How was that self-serving?"

"Maybe he's trying to cut a deal," Donnelly suggested. "He thinks the Fangs are going down, so he betrays them. Offers to trade knowledge for his life."

All shyness, all nervousness, had vanished from his 'meek' secretary. Fighting for his life, she found a new courage. One strong enough to contradict a Dragon. "That doesn't make sense. He didn't put any conditions on sharing info with us."

Donnelly snorted. "So, you're telling me that he's still going to spill the beans even if we decide to kill him?"

"Yes," Jordan said. "Savannah's right. I'm not bargaining for anything."

"Huh." The Dragon leaned back in his chair. "All right. That's one point for you."

"Oh, please!" Nose wrinkling with irritation, Witch Queen LePierre interrupted. "We're losing sight of the one indisputable fact that condemns him. The man is a Worm. A *Worm.* A debased, fallen Dragon. Tell me we are not seriously considering letting one of these creatures survive?"

For a moment, he had dared to hope that Savannah could

persuade them. But at the Hare's reprimand, faces around the room hardened. Wolves, Bears, and Dragons all grew darker.

The Rat, however, almost laughed. "Ain't that the truth?" SueSue chortled. "Worms! They're awful! Hell, they're as bad as Chimeras!"

That support, so unexpected, surprised Jordan. Was the old Rat an ally?

Her words certainly hit their target: Griffin Davis. The Chimera's frown melted away. "She's right. We *have* to judge him on his deeds, not his Kind."

The laser of the Hare's annoyance turned to him. Clearly the Witch Queen was *not* happy to have Rats and Chimeras yapping in the middle of *her* trial. "Kind and deed cannot be separated."

Anger flared in the shapeshifter's eyes. "I remember you saying almost that exact same thing about me at our last trial."

"This is why trials are shit!" King muttered. All three Wolf Alphas began to pace like trapped animals.

Stunned by the sudden change, Jordan felt a strange, alien emotion.

Hope. Could Savannah actually pull this off?

SueSue and Griffin would vote to acquit him, he was sure. The Dragons would probably condemn – unless Donnelly decided 'one point in his favor' was enough. LePierre was a definite no. The Bear hadn't said a word… but he was a good friend of SueSue. The old Rat had saved his family – and that was the greatest favor you could ever do for a Bear.

And the Wolves? Hell, the only thing they'd vote for now was a beer run.

Savannah – and SueSue – had split the room. One good speech, one more piece of evidence, in his favor… and the women might win his freedom.

His secretary was prepared. Proud and confident, she rose to her feet again. "I think the real question is–"

A gunshot shattered the night's stillness.

Jordan threw himself forward, tackling Savannah and covering her with his body. Around them, the room exploded into action. Wolves drew their guns and streamed out the door. Rex Fairborn Shifted into a hulking Kodiak Bear that loomed protectively over Queen LePierre. SueSue scurried close to him as Briggs and Davis followed the Wolves.

A shadow fell over Jordan and Savannah. The Worm looked up – into the face of Finn Donnelly.

Half-Shifted, he was fully armored in white scales. Three-inch-long talons curved from his fingers, strong enough to slice through steel.

Or a Worm.

That lethal arm was cocked back, frozen in mid-swing.

He thought I was trying to escape – or take a hostage.

Jordan felt a grudging respect for the old warrior.

That's a man who never forgets his enemy.

"Are you all right, Ms. Dare?" Sharp teeth slurred the Dragon's words.

As Jordan raised himself to one elbow, she gave a shaky nod. "Yes. What happened?"

A good question. Careful to keep his body between Savannah and any windows, Jordan scanned for threats. The Dragon, he ignored. Donnelly might not realize it but they were on the same side.

More noise came from outside. Aaron King backed in, pointing a gun at someone. Jordan rose to shield Savannah and was pleased to see that the white Dragon actually joined him.

Todd Manning, Savannah's handler, entered with his

hands raised. "Sorry for that, folks. I wish there'd been another way, but…"

Donnelly visibly relaxed. "Manning, what happened? King, it's okay. Manning's been handling espionage for the First Flight."

The Wolf's gun never wavered. "Now, he's shooting Rats."

"I shot a traitor. One who was trying to plant explosives under this building."

Murmurs broke out. King finally relented and holstered his weapon as people drifted back to their seats. Only SueSue Mint remained on her feet, close to the back door. Rex Fairburn shuffled over and nuzzled her, still in his Bear form. The Rat didn't seem comforted by that gesture.

"Please, let me explain." Sorrow radiated from Manning's broad face. A grief so strong it made Jordan suspicious. "Three days ago, Savannah Dare told me Nemo's true identity. I only shared that information with a handful of people. Yet two days later, the Fangs of Apophis knew. Someone told them. Someone high up in our ranks."

Jordan had wondered about that. Manning was still the chief suspect in his book, though. Today's events didn't improve his opinion of the man.

"I just found out who that was. Josh Bentley. My liaison with the local Rats."

All the blood drained from SueSue's face. "You shot Josh? King, is he dead?"

The Wolf nodded. "He is."

"I traced the leak back to him," Manning said. "When I went to confront him, I found him stuffing this under the house." He held up a small grey packet, wrapped in plastic. "Explosives. Enough to kill anyone except a Dragon."

"Liar!" SueSue's teeth chattered against each other, a sign of rage, which Rats rarely revealed. "I've known Josh since he was a pup. He'd never try to kill me."

"Ma'am, I'm sorry." Head bowed, Manning was a picture of sorrow. "I'd be happy to show you the paper trail that proves his guilt."

"Liar!"

"Ms. Mint, please." LePierre held up a delicate hand for silence.

"What? The man's a liar! Somebody ought to put a bullet in his brain."

Beside him, Savannah shivered – an unpleasant reminder that she'd been close to Manning. Jordan longed to slip an arm around her shoulders, but that would be grievously out of line. This wasn't a pain he could protect her from.

"You can prove these accusations?" Donnelly's last scales vanished as he frowned at the Bear.

"Yes, sir. I'll do that as soon as this trial is done, of course. I–"

"Liar!"

"Ms. Mint!" LePierre's Hare stomped a warning. "You are out of line!"

"I'm out of line?" the Rat cackled. "What about the asshole who killed Josh?"

Casey Briggs cleared his throat and added his vote to the doubters. "I know this is hard to accept, Ms. Mint. But Mr. Manning is correct: We clearly have a traitor in our midst."

"Well, how do you know it's not him?" She jerked a finger at the handler.

LePierre pursed her lips. "Todd Manning has served the First Flight and Sedona for years. I would never question his loyalty. I know he was a friend of yours, but Josh Bentley is a much more likely culprit because... well, he is," the Witch Queen finished lamely.

Jordan knew what she really meant.

So did SueSue. "Say it. 'Because he's a Rat.' That's what you meant."

"Ms. Mint…" Briggs held up a hand. "Please…"

But LePierre wasn't even apologetic. "Yes, that's what I meant. He was a Rat. Your Kind's reputation precedes you."

Harsh and brimming with contempt, SueSue's laughter echoed in the room. "Sure, it does. Worms and Chimeras and Rats. Everybody knows what we are!"

Fairburn Shifted human once more and shot the other Bear a burning glare. "SueSue, I'm sorry. Let's hear what–"

"No! I've heard enough." The old woman's eyes raked across the other Shifters. "Screw all of you. Screw you *and* your trial. I'm out of here."

She stormed out the back door, Fairburn in her wake futilely trying to calm her down.

Inside, Jordan cringed. This was why the Fangs were winning. The 'Good' Guys couldn't manage to be decent to each other. Prejudice ran deep in Shifter society.

LePierre rolled her eyes. "Idiots! Now, we don't have votes from the Bears *or* the Rats! And where are you three going?" She turned an outraged, baleful glare on the three Wolves.

King paused in the doorway. "I got a bottle of Jack Daniel's in my kit. Now, we gotta rustle up some beer to chase it down."

Ah, yes. The predicted beer run. Right on schedule.

"Sit down," the Witch Queen hissed. "We're not finished here."

That was the *wrong* tone to use with Wolf Alphas. King's voice dropped to a soft, dangerous purr. "Woman, get that sneer off your face, or I'll slap it off."

Safe in the presence of Dragons, the Hare gave little weight to his threat. "Oh, really? You're threatening to assault women now? Where's your Wolfish 'honor'?"

Good lord. Was *any* Kind immune to her scorn?

King's eyes narrowed, then he stuck his head out the door

and bellowed at the top of his lungs. "Lily! Get over here, girl. I got a woman who needs her ass kicked in the worst way."

Cheers rang out from the Wolf Packs and a young woman yelled, "Be right there, Pops!"

Briggs winced. "No. No, no, no, no, no…. Don't drag my Mate into this… A thousand pardons…" Before the Witch Hare could object, he bolted out the door. Closely followed by the three Wolves.

Which left only Griffin, Donnelly, and LePierre, Jordan noted. Well, and Manning. Nobody seemed inclined to give him the 'Bear' vote, though.

A tiny pool of voters. And *not* ones friendly to him.

LePierre flounced back in her chair with a dramatic sigh. "How typical. As always, Hares and Dragons remain the only responsible Shifters in our community."

"And Chimeras," Griffin added with a sweet smile. "Don't forget the Chimera."

"My apologies. Glad to see that you're not as easily insulted as our Rats and Wolves."

The 'sugar' in his smile curdled but his grin never disappeared. "Oh, don't get me wrong. You've insulted the hell out of me. Unlike the Rats and Wolves, though, the madder *I* get, the more I want to sit here and keep my vote. And my vote is to acquit."

Donnelly startled. "You think he can redeem himself?"

Jordan's long-time not-quite-a-friend shrugged. "I don't know. I think people deserve a second chance though. And that too many people have already died today. I'm not willing to kill more."

"Well *I* am," LePierre huffed. "I vote to convict."

Which meant the deciding vote fell to Donnelly – and Jordan had no doubt what the Dragon thought of him.

At least it will be quick.

"Mr. Donnelly?" LePierre prompted. "What is your vote?"

Shoulders slumped, the Dragon stared at Jordan. Thoughtful. Sad. Pensive.

None of that gave the Worm any hope. There was too much bad blood between their Kinds. Too much history. Too much death.

Donnelly knew it too, and in the end, he shook his head. "I'm sorry. You've done us a lot of good but, at the end of the day, you're a Worm. I can't let you go. I vote–"

"ENOUGH!"

Like a trumpet's clear blast, Savannah's voice silenced the room. "This farce needs to end, now! You!" One quick step brought her face to face with Donnelly, and the hulking Dragon shied away as she poked him in the chest. "I thought the whole point of this trial was democracy. Instead of Dragons giving orders, all the Kinds would be involved. We'd work things out together. Well, in case you didn't notice, only half of the Kinds are still here."

"They chose not to participate," LePierre snapped. "They left."

"They got driven out. By you," Savannah countered.

The Hare's eyes narrowed. "Kin-woman, you will keep a civil tongue in your head when you address Shifters."

"Hey." A menacing growl entered Donnelly's voice. One that echoed in Jordan's own heart. "No threats. This lady raises a good point. We need the others."

"Oh, please!" LePierre surged to her feet, throwing her arms wide. "Isn't today proof that your 'democracy' doesn't work? There is a natural hierarchy among Shifters, whether you want to admit it or not. Dragons, Hares, Bears... then Wolves and Rats."

"...cough... Chimeras... cough..." Griffin snorted.

"I think you're below 'the Hierarchy' with us Worms," Jordan said in a stage whisper.

Ignoring the Hare, Savannah peered up into Donnelly's

face. "Listen to yourselves. Is that really the world you want? Where Dragons are kings, Hares advise them… and all the rest of us are peasants?"

"Lady, you're Kin." A nasty humor curled Griffin's lip. "You don't even rate as high as a peasant."

"Mock all you like." The Hare's eyes narrowed to two furious slits. "However, that form of rule has served us well for centuries. Today demonstrates why. Mr. Donnelly, I ask you again: What is your vote?"

The Dragon sighed. "Look, I've got an idea. Why don't we try this again tomorrow? This time, I'll bring my Mate. Bree is *great* with people and–"

"You need your Mate to tell you what you think?" LePierre sneered.

Red light blazed in the Dragon's eyes. "ENOUGH."

Savannah's shout had been a trumpet; Donnelly's was as loud as an air raid siren. Even Jordan found himself flinching away from his wrath.

"You want a king? Fine. Here's what the king orders. You!" he snapped at Manning. "Get your damned evidence in order because you need to persuade me you're not a murderer. Bring it to my hotel in one hour."

"You!" Savannah squeaked as his burning gaze swung to her. "Go home. Rest. You've earned it."

"You!" LePierre blanched but glared back. "Get out there and apologize to everyone you pissed off. We're reconvening tomorrow at noon. If anyone doesn't show up, I hold *you* responsible."

"You!" By the time Donnelly waved a finger at Jordan, the Worm could see that his flash of temper had already dimmed. Pretty levelheaded – for a Dragon. "You come with me. Tonight, you tell me and Briggs everything you know about the Fangs."

His scowl circled the now-silent room. "Everybody clear?"

Griffin cleared his throat. "Once again, the Chimeras have been forgotten, consigned to the dust-bin of history."

"You," Donnelly snorted. "Go do whatever Chimeras do."

"Mostly, we steal things and assassinate people."

"Whatever. I'm not going to micro-manage you." Already, the man was back to his usual jokes. Once everyone had their 'orders', the Dragon swept out.

Leaving Jordan no chance to say goodbye to Savannah. He longed to kiss her before they left. To tell her, with both body and words, how much she meant to him. Whether she knew it or not, she'd saved his life.

Again.

CHAPTER 11

"Go home," Finn Donnelly had told her.

Easier said than done.

After three years working undercover in the Fangs, Savannah didn't *have* a home. The First Flight paid for a lovely suite in one of Sedona's many resorts. It came with a balcony, Jacuzzi, gym, and swimming pool. Honestly, though, the only amenity she cared about was room service. Order a sandwich, a bottle of wine, and flop on the couch after getting changed into…

Nothing. All her clothes were at her old apartment. Which, no doubt, the Fangs had torn apart by this point.

Oh well. The room came with a bathrobe, and the wine was lovely. She'd survive. Tomorrow, she could start to rebuild her life.

After the second stage of the trial. *After* she gave Jordan Beaumont a chance to rebuild his life too.

Where was her 'master' now? Swirling her wine, she stared out at the moonlit desert. A deep melancholy swept over her. Was he in a prison, with two enemy Dragons watching him like a hawk, ready to kill him in a heartbeat if he made a single 'suspicious' move?

The thought kindled a fire within her, an anger that burned away that soul-killing grief. Why the hell were Shifters so blind? Didn't they see his kindness? A gun goes off, and his first thought was of her. Not himself. Not escape. Protecting *her*. Didn't that show his true nature; that, deep down, he was a good man?

True, he was a Worm. As Kin, she knew what that meant. But she had to believe in redemption. In second chances. Without that, everyone was doomed.

We all make mistakes. We must be given the opportunity to fix the messes we make.

On the table, her phone buzzed.

Todd. Again. This was the fourth time he'd called in the last hour. His meeting with the First Flight must have gone okay.

That should have pleased her. Her lover wasn't a murderer.

Yay.

Damn. Savannah sipped her wine, shocked by her own coldness.

What the hell is wrong with me? I'm sitting here, wound to hell about the fate of some Worm and I couldn't care less about my own boyfriend.

Maybe that was because that 'Worm' treated her a hell of a lot better than her 'boyfriend' ever did.

There. That was the truth. A fact she'd refused to see for two years.

I was so flattered that a Bear, a Shifter, would 'fall' for a mere Kin like me that I was blinded.

To Todd's selfishness; his willingness to risk her life; the way he belittled her and ordered her about.

I don't feel loved when I'm with him. I feel... well, like an ingrate. A silly Kin woman who doesn't appreciate how lucky she is to have a lover like him.

She remembered Todd's cutting words this afternoon, embarrassing her in front of the entire Shifter council.

And how Jordan Beaumont had leaped to her defense.

He did that a lot. Even deep in the heart of Ormaz Corp., he made her office a tiny fortress. The one safe place where she could retreat. He defended her, refused to allow others to put her down. It didn't matter if her attackers were Fangs or Shifters. There was no man he wouldn't battle on her behalf.

Warmth filled her at that thought, a gentle happiness. Nothing had ever made her feel so loved in all her life.

Love? What a silly, overwrought word to use! Jordan Beaumont didn't love her. He just… just…

The phone's shrill ring demanded her attention. She ignored the request.

No, Todd. Not tonight. Why the hell couldn't the man take a hint?

The sharp annoyance that filled her made one thing plain, however. She didn't know how Jordan felt about her, what word could describe the awkward, delightful, strange bond between them.

But, whatever it was, it was a hell of a lot better than what she and Todd shared.

Savannah tilted her glass back, letting the last of the wine swirl across her tongue.

Tomorrow, her world would change. She would learn the fate of the man for whom she'd come to care. One chapter of her life would close – and she had no idea what she wanted to 'write' in the next one.

One thing was clear though. It was time to write Todd out of her life and see if there was a place for Jordan Beaumont instead.

Tonight, though, sleep. She needed her strength for the battles of the next day.

A whispered plea woke Savannah from a deep sleep – and into a dream.

...help me...

She lay on an autumn moor. Dried, dead grass rose high above her. When she stood, she found herself amid desolation. Grey sky overhead, thick clouds that wrapped the world in twilight. An endless sea of dead vegetation stretched in all directions.

In the distance, lay something darker. A lake of black, peat-stained waters. No breeze stirred its dead, ebony surface.

...help me...

Once more, there was that plea, from somewhere near the lake. Savannah dusted herself off and strode toward it.

She wore nothing except a long white shift. Her arms and feet lay bared to the chill air. Dead grass crunched underfoot, its frost-touched blades seeking to tear her feet. Yet the cold couldn't harm her. A heat – rich and strong – radiated off her body. It held the cold at bay and turned aside the moor's feeble attacks.

At the water's edge, she found a tiny rowboat. No one else was there, and that cry for aid never repeated itself. After a moment, she stepped into the boat and took a seat.

Like in the dream with the dragonfly, Savannah marveled at the vivid details. The scent of rot, thick in the air. The dampness of the boat's floorboards against her feet. The faint whish of water against its bow as the boat arrowed deeper into the lake, driven by unseen hands.

That makes two of these strange dreams. It can't be a coincidence. I need to ask a Hare what this means!

Not Witch Queen LePierre, however. There was no way she would ask that woman for help!

At the center of the lake, the boat drifted to a halt. Savannah studied the waters, seeking clues as to why it had brought her here. Streamers of mist drifted across the surface, dark and haunting.

Nothing, as far as the eye could see. She leaned over the boat's edge and peered down into the water.

Something stirred in the depths. Something pale that drifted toward the surface. Instinct screamed at her to recoil as the ghostly form rose closer, but Savannah gritted her teeth and held her ground.

A woman's face rose into view, surrounded by billows of long hair. Where her eyes should be were two black holes and her pale skin had a sickly, yellowish cast.

"Hello? Did you call for help?"

"…yes…" the form burbled.

It sounded nothing like the voice that had summoned her. Yet, even in her dreams, she wasn't willing to abandon anyone. "What's wrong? How can I help?"

"Laud… laudanum…lauda… g-give me…"

Laudanum? Wasn't that some old Victorian drug? "I'm sorry, I don't have any."

Rage swept across the vision's face. Thin lips curled back from her teeth and she screamed, "Liar! You took it all yourself! You let me suffer while you… while you… GIVE IT TO ME!"

"I swear, I don't have any laudanum. Why don't you tell me who you are and I'll–"

"I'm your *wife!*" Two bony hands lashed out of the water and fastened onto the side of the boat. The little dinghy rocked sharply, threatening to dump Savannah into the cold water. "Give it to me! I can still hear them!"

Then Savannah heard 'them' too. Children calling from the mists. "Mommy! Daddy! Where are you?"

"Give it to me!" Savannah lurched as the drowned woman began to drag herself into the boat. "I can't hear them when I have it. Give me the laudanum, you bastard!"

The surface of the lake roiled. An enormous form, long and sinuous like a sea serpent, writhed. Savannah caught a glimpse of black scales, glistening in the water. Ghostly forms clung to it, hissing a litany of accusations. "You lied! You betrayed me! You left! You never loved me!"

At once, the drowned woman abandoned the boat. She shot through the water and grabbed the serpent, adding her complaint to all the others: "You took all the laudanum!"

Weighed down by all those bodies, the serpent sank, once more, beneath the waves. But as it disappeared, Savannah heard a voice in her head.

…help me…

Stillness returned, and with it, shock.

This wasn't a dream. This was real. A spiritual realm she'd entered in her sleep.

That form? That was a Dragon. The dead, decaying remnant of Jordan Beaumont's Shifter soul.

Begging her for help.

And the wraiths that haunted these waters?

Those must be the people he loved. The ones he failed to protect.

All was clear… except for one thing.

What should she do? *How* could she help him?

"Jordan!" On unsteady feet, she stood and waved at the Dragon. "These aren't memories. They're your guilt, not the truth. You still have good in you."

Nothing broke the silence. Well, perhaps a warmer heart could win where mere words failed?

She thought of today's meeting and how Jordan's first thought was for her safety. The way he shielded her with his own body. The joy that brought her, to know a man would risk himself for her.

A soft, pearly light spread along her hands. She was beginning to glow, her body shining a pale light across the dark waters. Delighted, she added more memories. The way Jordan kicked down the lunchroom door to save her from that Darkborn. How he kept close to her, guarding her, as they left Ormaz.

"You remember what it means to be a Dragon," she whispered to the lake. "You can be one again."

Light surrounded her now, sharp and strong in the grey. Yet, no matter how it grew, it did not call Jordan's soul to the surface. Only the ghosts came, pale strands of slime in the dark water. Angry, hungry. The light kept them at bay; none dared touch the boat. They longed to, though. To flip the boat and drag her under. Devour the light, the devotion, that her own soul held.

More light. More love. That's what she needed. So, she thought of poor Lara, and how upset Jordan was when...

"...when he failed to save me. Like he's failed everyone else."

Lara floated among the other dead, purple hair faded, mascara smeared across her face. A bloodless bullet hole in the center of her forehead.

The sight of that familiar corpse chilled Savannah, but she wouldn't give up. "Eddy shot you. Your death is his fault, not Jordan's."

"He tried to save me and failed," the secretary whispered. "He failed."

She hadn't known Lara well – well enough to be sure that *wasn't* right. "You aren't real. The *real* Lara would be pissed as hell that her lover and master didn't think she was worth a five-minute wait." Dragging her eyes away from the woman's corpse, she called out across the waters. "Jordan, that's not

Lara. That's you. Your guilt. You can't blame yourself for her death."

But he did. The ghosts of the lake were proof of how deep his guilt ran.

"I don't blame you."

Nothing. No movement, no sound, except the ghosts' quiet complaints.

And suddenly, she understood what was wrong. Words held no power here. Only deeds mattered. Her path became clear to her and she set her feet upon it with a calm, sure heart. "I trust you! I know you remember your true self. Let me prove it to you."

One step. She placed her bare foot on the edge of the boat – and it flipped. Casting her into the dark lake... and the arms of its wraiths.

Water closed over her head. The light that shone from her body, so soft and comforting, vanished, quenched by that chill touch. Her white shift wrapped about her legs like a corpse's shroud.

Then, they came. Jordan's dead. Snatching at her, their bony fingers twining through her hair. Pressing close, dragging her into the depths. Hissing with vicious delight.

And nowhere, *nowhere*, was there any sign of Jordan.

Deeper, she sank, lungs burning. Savannah gasped in pain as fingernails raked her leg, and boggy water rushed in to fill her mouth.

"You'll see," Lara promised as she tugged her to her doom. "No one's going to save you. No one ever gets saved."

Savannah gagged, choked. Feebly, she fought to claw her way to the surface. The ghosts were right. This was a mistake.

And then, the ground rushed up toward her.

No, not the ground. A vast serpent, rising from the

depths. Catching her, boiling upward with her secure in its claws.

As they broke the surface, it sought the sky. But the 'wings' that spread from its back were bones and tatters of skin. They beat furiously – and impotently – against the air. Shamed, the creature limped to shore, carefully holding her above the waters. There, it set her down gently among the dried grasses.

Drenched and shivering, Savannah staggered to her feet.

It was a Dragon. Or, the remains of one. Weeds draped across its muck-spattered scales. Bones poked through its gaunt form and the skeletal ruins of its wings trailed beside it.

It was hideous… horrible…

But a Dragon. *Not* a Worm.

"I told you," she whispered, as a fit of coughing took her. "I told you."

…knock knock knock…

The dream shimmered, threatening to dissolve.

"You saved me. You remember. You can–"

…KNOCK KNOCK KNOCK!…

Thundering and insistent, that sound dragged her back into the waking world.

With a wail of disappointment, Savannah sat up in her resort bed.

…knock knock knock KNOCK KNOCK…

It was 2:15 am. Who could that be? Was there a fire? Had the Fangs found her?

Still groggy and dazed, Savannah staggered over to the door's peephole.

A familiar man stood outside her door in the middle of the night.

"Todd?"

"Savannah. Open the door. We need to talk."

CHAPTER 12

"What's wrong?" Adrenaline mixed with the remnants of the dream – and all that did was leave her fuzzy-headed. "Has there been an attack?"

"What? No. I just wanted to talk to you."

"At two in the morning?" Was he drunk? Savannah squinted through the peephole, but the Bear seemed steady on his feet.

Just annoyed. "Yes, at two. The damned Dragons grilled me for hours. I got here as soon as I could."

He sounded so irritated. Like Josh Bentley had seriously inconvenienced him by 'demanding' to be shot. "Let's talk in the morning, all right? I'm really tired."

"Seriously? I thought you'd want to talk after what happened."

After *what* happened? Savannah didn't know if it was fatigue or annoyance that clouded her mind, but she could *not* understand what he meant. Why would she want to talk about Bentley's death? Todd was the one who killed him. Or did her handler worry that she wasn't strong enough to do her job?

"Is this about me shooting Mariset? If so, I'm okay with it." She'd never actually killed anyone – but every spy knows that, one day, they might be forced to make that lethal choice."

"What? No! I meant after you embarrassed me in front of all the senior Shifters of this region."

Oh. When she refused to obey his orders. When he yelled at her like a disobedient pet. "Todd…"

"Why are we still talking through this goddamn door? Are you going to let me in, or what?"

'Or what' was *very* tempting right now. Though there was no way in hell she'd sleep again tonight. Not after this argument and that dream.

Two a.m. breakup… in a bath robe. Sure. Why not?

Sighing, she opened the door. Todd brushed past her and scanned the room with deep suspicion, as if he expected to see another man's feet sticking out from under the couch.

"Coffee?"

"No."

Good. Because there were only two packets left and she was sure she'd need both.

Hot, angry eyes studied her as she crossed the room. Intent on getting her caffeine, Savannah ignored him.

"Well?" Todd snapped at last.

"Well what?" Man, this had to be the slowest coffeemaker on the planet!

"I expect an apology."

"So do I," she shot back. "I bet we're both going to be disappointed."

"What the hell did I do wrong?"

"You ordered me about like a dog. You treated me like a child, not a skilled undercover agent."

"And you forgot yourself! You're the agent. *I'm* the handler. I *am* in charge."

"Respect still matters."

"Are you kidding me?" he scoffed. "You were permitted to speak before the leaders of the Shifter community. That's more respect than any Kin woman should hope for."

And there it was. Savannah took a sip of the black coffee, letting its bitterness join the darkness in her heart. That was the truth. The fact that doomed their relationship from the start. Todd would never consider her his equal. Without respect, love had no chance.

I shouldn't have fallen for a Shifter. They're all jerks.

No, not all of them. Jordan Beaumont never looked down his nose at her. Physically, he was far more powerful. Yet, he respected *her*. Her intelligence. Her wit. Her heart.

Todd didn't.

Because he's an asshole, not a Shifter.

An asshole who wasn't done grousing. "You have to remember how the world works. When you insult me in front of my peers—"

"Todd, stop." She didn't need to raise her voice. The disgust on her face silenced him. "There's no point arguing about this. We're done."

His jaw dropped in almost comical shock. "You're breaking up with me?"

What was he…? Oh.

Well, that wasn't the most tactful way of saying it, but… "I meant, professionally. I won't be taking a second undercover job, so you aren't my handler anymore. But… yes. I do want to break up."

"Seriously? Just like that? No talk? Not even going to bother to try to fix it?"

"You said I'm not your equal. I'm 'just' Kin. What else is there to talk about? I can't 'fix' that."

"That's hardly a surprise! From the start, we both knew you were Kin."

"But I didn't know what that meant to you." Tears stung her eyes, sudden and unexpected. Savannah didn't know how she'd ever cared for this man… but she had. "I thought you saw me as a partner, not a pet."

"Bullshit." His eyes narrowed as he rose to his feet. "You're seeing someone else, aren't you?"

"What? No!"

"You are. Who… Oh, hell, tell me it's not that stinking Worm? If you picked a goddamn Worm over me, I will…"

That 'goddamn' Worm cares about me! He protects me! He stands up for me when jerks like you insult me!

No point saying any of that, though. It would only drive the Bear berserk.

"Tell me you didn't sleep with that goddamn Worm!"

"I did not cheat on you," she snapped. "I did not sleep with my boss. Happy?"

Todd rocked on his heels as if he could feel, physically, the waves of anger rolling over him. Quickly, though, that rage vanished.

Very quickly. Like, one second later. Savannah blinked, stunned by how fast he came to terms with the breakup and sighed, "Oh well. Like you say, it doesn't matter."

He really didn't care about me.

Once again, pain lanced through her heart. At least, she consoled herself, that would make their parting easier.

"Saves me time too." From under his jacket, Todd drew a .357.

And pointed it at her.

Her heart skipped a beat. "Todd, what are you doing?"

"Cleaning up a loose end. The real reason I came over was to find out your plans for the future. Getting an apology before you died was just icing on the cake."

Everything fell into place now. Why he never worried

about her safety. Why he refused to ask Griffin and Ghost what Jordan had told them.

Why the Fangs knew her boss was Nemo the moment she told Todd.

"No need to schedule some 'accident' in the future." He clicked the safety off, his hand steady as a rock. "Apparently, the Fangs of Apophis found you and killed you."

Ironically, they actually had. Heart hammering, Savannah ran through her escape routes. The door behind her was locked. There was a great view from the balcony – and a four-story drop to the ground.

No way out. So, stall. Keep talking. Keep looking for an opportunity.

"You work for the Fangs, don't you? *You* told them who Nemo was. Josh Bentley must have found that out." She felt a flash of pride at her calm, steady voice. If Todd expected her to weep, scream, or beg, he would be sadly disappointed.

"Congrats. Figured that out a little too late, though."

"That must be why you–"

"Savannah, Savannah." The disdain in his chuckle grated. "No more stalling. 'We' end, here and now."

CHAPTER 13

Six hours before that knock on Savannah's door, Jordan surveyed his latest 'prison' with dry amusement. Only the best for a Dragon.

Finn Donnelly's penthouse hotel suite came with its own patio, complete with a hot tub and panoramic views out over the desert. Living room, dining room, and three full bedrooms.

It was the finest prison Jordan had ever been in. Couldn't ask for a better place to spend his last night on Earth.

The entertainment left something to be desired, however. Donnelly and Briggs escorted him here after the trial. One of them stayed with him at every step. He didn't intend to escape, but if he had any such delusion, the two Dragons squelched it. As soon as they arrived, Donnelly began to interrogate him about the Fangs of Apophis. Who was in charge. Where their facilities were. What plots they had brewing.

Jordan told him everything he knew, holding nothing back.

"You weren't kidding when you said you'd help us, were

you?" A grudging respect warmed Donnelly's words. "Can't swear it'll help you at tomorrow's trial but, well, I appreciate it."

One hour later, Todd Manning arrived – just as he'd been ordered. The Bear clutched a thick folder. Presumably, the evidence he planned to present to prove Josh Bentley's guilt.

Donnelly leaned back with his arms stretched along the back of the couch. A friendly, relaxed posture – and one completely at odds with the suspicious glint in the Dragon's eyes. "Let's hear it."

Todd paused, frowning at Jordan. "Shouldn't he be somewhere else?"

"Nope. I want him right here where I can see him."

"But he's a Fang. Some of this information touches upon our spy network and–"

"Look, tomorrow, Beaumont's either going to be dead or one of us. So, say what you have to say."

Rendered speechless by the other Dragon's lack of subtlety, Manning just kept blinking. Jordan, however, found it refreshing.

The man lets you know exactly where you stand.

Obedient, Manning presented his evidence.

And got grilled. For three intense, grueling hours. Every one of his points withstood the scrutiny, but the Bear's shirt was soaked in sweat by the time the Dragons finished with him.

In the end, Donnelly squinted at the clock. "Thank you. Didn't mean to run this to almost midnight, but I trust you understand."

"Of course, sir. Of course." Manning mopped his forehead with his sleeve.

"You'll be at the trial tomorrow, yes?"

"Yes, sir."

"Good. We'll talk tomorrow night about where we go now."

"Thank you." Hands were shaken, pleasantries were exchanged. Manning retreated and left the three of them sitting in silence.

A stillness that lasted for three minutes, until Donnelly turned to Jordan and said, "So, what did you think of that?"

The Worm chuckled. "I assume you ask because I, as a former Fang of Apophis, am the resident expert in treachery?"

"Right in one."

Under better circumstances, he could like this Dragon. "The man's lying. I can't prove that, but he reads wrong. Too nervous. Too well prepared."

"I felt much the same," Briggs interjected.

"I can see a couple spots where his story might fall apart. Talk to Ghost of the Sand Pack. Manning says those emails prove Bentley was a traitor. Well, electronic data can be faked. Ghost will tell you if they're real. Also, I'd talk to SueSue Mint."

Donnelly grimaced. "Might be hard to find her now."

"Rats do tend to hide after one of their own gets killed. But Ms. Mint is Rex Fairburn's babysitter. I'm sure he can get in touch with her."

"What purpose would that serve, though?" Briggs asked.

"Manning claimed that Bentley was going to blow up the trial room, and he had the C-4 explosives to 'prove' it. Well, you don't just pick that stuff up at Home Depot. This trial came out of the blue. No warning. Our saboteur only had a couple hours to prepare for it, which is nowhere near enough time to get a bunch of explosives shipped from the Fangs. Whoever he is, the guy got that C-4 himself. SueSue Mint's a Rat. She knows the black market around here, and where you'd make that kind of purchase."

Donnelly nodded. "If we find the seller, we find out who he sold it to."

"He might not have names, but even a mortal would notice the physical differences between a Bear and a Rat."

The Dragon squinted at him. "You're pretty good with this treachery stuff."

"It *is* a prerequisite for surviving in the Fangs."

Another glance at the clock. Now it *was* midnight. Strange, he didn't feel tired, not even after the day's events. An odd tension had seized him, a fit of very uncharacteristic nerves.

Briggs, however, stifled a yawn.

"Why don't I take the first watch?" Donnelly suggested.

Right. This was still a prison, no matter how comfortable it might be. The black Dragon retired, leaving just the two of them.

"Door stays open when you go to bed," Donnelly said. "No offense, but I want to keep an eye on you."

The thought of sleep made his skin actually crawl. It would be… a sin. Remiss… There was something he ought to be doing.

All of which were foolish thoughts, vapors he would *not* share with the Dragon. "I'm not tired. Why don't I continue my report on the Fangs?"

"Fine by me. I'm going to be up all night. Well, until Briggs gets his beauty sleep."

The interrogation distracted Jordan for a time. Yet his unease remained, lurking beneath the questions. A nagging feeling, as if he was failing. Failing someone again.

I owe no loyalty to the Fangs. I cannot possibly blame myself for betraying them.

By quarter to 2:00, even Donnelly noticed. "You okay? You're fidgeting like… well, like an addict who's overdue for his next fix. Tell me you're not a junkie…"

"No. Not in... well, over a century. But..."

"But?" The Dragon leaned forward, full attention on him.

"But..." No point trying to save his dignity. Donnelly already knew something was amiss. "Do you sense anything?"

"Like?"

"I don't know. Something wrong. Something... something's not right."

"You gotta be more specific than that."

"Magic, maybe?"

Donnelly snorted. "I'm no Hare. I wouldn't sense magic if Doc Strange himself stood in front of me and blasted me in the face. Do you want me to get someone from Sedona?"

At 2:00 am? "No, that's not necessary. It would be foolish."

"What's foolish is ignoring facts," the Dragon countered. "Describe *exactly* what you're feeling."

Dammit, this was embarrassing! "I feel as though something is wrong. There's something I ought to be doing, something important, and I'm not. I'm failing."

"Failing who?"

"No idea."

"Doesn't sound like a 'Come Hither' spell. Any other nasty Fang magics you know about?"

In his anxiety, he'd completely forgotten about the spell, one that let a Hare summon their victim to their doom. "No spells that will affect a person at a distance, no."

"Hmm. When did this start?"

"A couple hours ago. Right after Manning left."

For some reason, that answer made the Dragon frown. "Do you want to go someplace?"

"You mean for a beer or something? I think the resort's bar is closed."

"No, not for beers. Stop thinking, just feel. Do you *feel* like you need to go someplace?"

Jordan's first instinct was to scoff. Yet when he stilled his restless mind, he *did* feel a tug. An urge to get up and leave. "Oh hell, maybe this *is* a Summoning!"

"Where do you want to go?"

"That way." He pointed off in a direction that meant nothing to him.

"Why?"

"I don't know!" he snapped. "I just feel like something… like *life* would be better if I was out there. Safer."

"Huh." Both men stared into the darkness. Lights sparkled in the distance where Jordan had pointed. Other hotels and resorts, no doubt, gleaming in the night.

"This has to be a Summoning. Fortunately, those are easy to resist once you've noticed them."

"Or…" A sly grin spread across Donnelly's broad face. "I could wake Briggs up and the three of us could follow your Summons. Give the Fangs at the other end one hell of a surprise!"

"They'll be prepared to take down a Worm."

"That just means it'll be a big fight!" The delight on his face made Jordan want to chuckle. The man truly was as excitable as a mastiff that–

Without warning, the world dropped out from beneath him. A primal need tore through him, so strong, so irresistible that it almost felt like terror. And a voice he had not heard in over a century suddenly rang in his head.

WE NEED TO GO NOW! SHE IS IN DANGER!

Jordan didn't need to ask who 'she' was.

Savannah.

Our Mate!

"No!" he screamed. Donnelly shied away from him, shocked by the outburst. "I have to go!"

"Beaumont, wait! Get a hold of yourself! It's a spell."

"No!" The word came out as a long, drawn out hiss.

Power washed over him, the touch of a spirit he thought long dead. Under its touch, his body grew. Skin hardened into scales, claws and fangs sprouted. "I am leaving!"

"Briggs!" Donnelly bellowed. "Get out here, now!"

He grabbed Jordan's arm as he summoned his own Dragon.

Without a thought, the Worm backhanded him. A casual blow that sent the Dragon flying through the air and slamming into the wall.

Then, he was running, crying out to his Shifter soul, and from the darkest recesses of his heart, his Dragon answered. One step and he dropped to all four. A great, serpentine tail unfurled. Razor-sharp talons dug into the patio and he threw himself over the edge. As Donnelly scrambled to his feet, Jordan leaped into the air, wings spreading wide.

No, not wings.

Bones, with scraps of leathery flesh clinging to them.

For too long, his Dragon had rotted in despair. Now, when he finally needed it, it could not help him. Nothing mattered more to a Dragon than its Mate, and his Dragon longed – with every inch of its heart – to fly to Savannah's rescue.

But it couldn't. Tattered shreds beat feebly at the air as his Dragon fought to fly by will alone.

It wasn't enough. Jordan plummeted, flailing past six floors, and slammed into the ground.

The impact cracked the pavement and set off every car alarm in the parking lot. Yet, enough of his Dragon's power remained to shield him from that drop. He staggered to his feet, ignoring the shrill wails.

The fall didn't matter. His wings didn't matter.

Only Savannah. And he still knew where she was.

Out into the desert, he galloped, cacti and thorns shattering against his thick scales. They tore at the shreds of his wings, a feeble attack he paid no mind.

Nothing would distract him. Nothing would stop him.

Overhead, wings beat the air, slow and heavy. Donnelly, probably. Or he and Briggs both.

No time to explain. Words meant delay, and delay was death. He dodged, hoping to throw his pursuers off.

But a Dragon in the air was the world's most deadly predator. Donnelly stooped, dropping from the sky like a hawk. The white Dragon plowed into his back with the force of a freight train. The blow slammed Jordan into the ground and drove the air from his lungs.

Frantic to escape, to save his Mate, he snapped at his captor. But Donnelly had him pinned, dagger-sized fangs mere inches from Jordan's neck. In Marakeen, the ancient tongue of Dragons, he hissed, "Resist! It's a spell! You're stronger than it!"

"No!" he shrieked in the same language; one he'd thought forgotten. "My Mate is in danger! My Mate!"

Shocked, the white Dragon reared back. For one moment, the grip of his claws weakened. That was the mistake Jordan needed. With a swift, fluid motion, he writhed, bucking Donnelly off. Then he leaped to his feet, once more tearing off as fast as he could.

Fast but not faster than a flying Dragon.

This time, Donnelly swept by, close overhead. Briggs flanked him. The white Dragon banked and dropped to the ground ahead of the fleeing Worm.

He wanted a fight? So be it! Jordan would destroy both of them, if that was what it took to save Savannah!

For once in his life, though, Donnelly wasn't looking for battle. "Shift! I will carry you!"

Shift? Abandon his scales, his only protection against a

Dragon's fangs and claws? Put his life – literally – in Donnelly's hands?

To save her? Yes! Neither Jordan nor his Worm hesitated. He cast his power aside, shrinking down into his frail human form.

Defenseless, he faced the two Dragons, ready for his fate, whatever it might be.

As gentle as a mother cat, Donnelly picked him up. Talons that could shred a bus curled harmlessly against his body. Then, on strong wings that sent dust billowing out around them, he rose into the air. Carrying the Worm safely.

Toward his Mate.

CHAPTER 14

Staring down the barrel of Todd's gun, Savannah felt her senses sharpen. Every detail of the room leaped into focus. The soft carpet underfoot. The reflection of Todd's gun in the picture's glass frame.

The steadiness of his hand, untroubled by any doubt, as he began to pull the trigger.

And then, the balcony's glass door exploded, and the world became a blur of motion.

A man had hurtled through the thick glass and rolled to his feet behind Todd. Dark scales, claws... a Dragon, half-Shifted into his mortal form.

The Bear spun and raised his weapon. In a blur of movement, the newcomer slashed...

...and a wave of blood sprayed across the room.

Todd Manning, one-time lover and now assassin, crumbled, dead, to the floor.

Black Dragon... that's Casey Briggs, right?

She stared at him, partially from shock. Partially to avoid looking at the crimson pool spreading along the white carpet.

Then, the Dragon finished his Shift – and Jordan Beaumont stood before her, wild-eyed, vigilant for any new enemy. "Savannah! Are you all right?"

"I f-fine. Fine, I…"

Her gaze kept dropping to that stain. How on Earth could anyone ever get that clean?

What a silly thing to think! What's wrong with me?

But she knew. The ringing in her ears gave it away, and the way she wobbled on her feet.

I'm in shock. I need to sit down before I faint.

Jordan rushed to her side, though, and wrapped his arms around her. Lending her the strength she needed to keep her feet under her. "You're pale. Sit down."

"Not here," she whispered. "Please, not here."

In the end, she grieved his death, even if he had tried to kill her. Savannah wasn't sure if she mourned Todd or the man she'd thought he was. Didn't matter. She just wanted to flee as far away as she could.

HER WORD WAS JORDAN'S COMMAND.

Finn Donnelly and Casey Briggs arrived a moment later, Shifting mid-air and dropping to the balcony with thuds that made the room shake. Briggs stayed to 'take care' of the mess. Donnelly got a cab and whisked them to another room back at his resort.

Jordan stayed by her the whole time. His arm, warm and steady, never left her shoulders. No sigh, no shiver, escaped his notice. He guarded her with a fierce attention she'd never seen before.

Like a Dragon.

Like the Dragon he used to be.

Donnelly's resort was a big, luxurious step up from hers. Jordan whisked her over to the couch. Only once she was settled and off her feet did he release his watchful hold. "Can I get you anything? Wine? Water?"

"Just water for now, please."

He hurried over to the kitchen (yes, this place actually had its own!). As he did, Donnelly ducked his head. "I'll be upstairs if you need me."

He was… leaving them alone? Leaving a prisoner free without a guard?!?

The shock must have been plain on her face because the Dragon snorted. "Ms. Dare, a little piece of advice. Next time, just *tell* the court that this guy is your Mate."

Mate.

The word stunned her, and her jaw dropped. "Mate? We're not, uh…"

Just like that, every trace of friendliness vanished from the Dragon's face. He whirled toward the kitchen, his blue eyes blazing as he called on his Dragon's power. "Beaumont, what the hell are you playing at?"

No answering fire lit Jordan's eyes, but his chin rose in defiance. "Nothing. Savannah Dare is my Mate. I know that now."

"But *she* doesn't?" Donnelly's eyes narrowed.

"Oh!" Savannah's mind spun. That mad, wonderful passion – they'd truly shared it? "Those dreams… they were real?"

Somber, the Worm nodded. "They were."

"But I thought…"

Donnelly's delighted cackle interrupted her. The Dragon's cheer had returned, in full force. "Gotcha. So, no treachery here, just stupidity. Ha! Lots of that going around."

"You will *not* refer to my Mate as 'stupid'!" Now, the anger returned, turning Jordan's emerald eyes into molten gems.

At once, Donnelly backed down. "Sorry, ma'am. I know better than to bark at someone's Mate. What I *should* have said is, the Rite of Claiming confuses a lot of people, not just you. I can see why you wouldn't assume a Worm could Claim a Mate anyway."

"Apology accepted."

"Good." With one last nod to Jordan, he backed out the door. "And on that note, I'm out of here. I'll pick you two up in the morning."

As Donnelly's heavy tread retreated down the hall, Jordan sighed. "I'm sorry. I should have asked."

"Asked what?"

"If I could stay with you."

"Of course, you can! You're my Mate."

'Mate.' How strange, how wonderful, that word felt on her tongue. Savannah still couldn't wrap her head around it fully. She was a Dragon's Mate. A very wounded Dragon, certainly. Not that it mattered. To her.

For him, it was a different story. "I'm sorry for that too. That had to be the most pathetic excuse for a 'Rite of Claiming' the world has ever seen. No cup, no dagger... I don't blame you for not realizing what it was. Hell, I didn't."

In Kin-folk legends, the Rite of Claiming was always so glamorous. Surrounded by a gorgeous dreamscape, Dragon and Mate revealed their souls to each other. By that act of truth and trust, they bound their souls for all time. Then, amid the wildest luxury and beauty they could imagine, they made love.

What did I get? A beat-up dragonfly and rummaging through a pile of bones.

Though the sex *had* been everything the stories promised! No complaints on that score.

In fact, did she have *any* true complaints? Her Dragon was a wounded soul, so badly injured that most Shifters wouldn't call him a 'Dragon' at all. Any Rite was a miracle; a flawless one seemed too much to hope for.

After all, what's more important? A big ring and an exotic destination wedding... or the love you bring to your marriage?

Savannah knew the answer to that, and her heart's contentment dispelled any shreds of disappointment she felt. "We got the Dragon equivalent of a quick trip to the justice of the peace rather than a full church wedding. So what? We're still Mates. That's all that matters."

"You set the bar very low. Though, I suppose I should be grateful for that. If you didn't, a Worm like me never would have passed muster."

"Stop it," she growled, giving him a little shake. "I'm Bear Kin. Bears don't brood – and they don't let their Mates brood either."

"Yes ma'am." Jordan gave her a mock salute, but the melancholy shadow that had shrouded his face faded away. "You probably want to get back to bed. I'll take the couch if that will make it easier for you to sleep."

At that suggestion, she burst out laughing. "You think I want to sleep? My boyfriend of two years just tried to murder me, and I found out that I was Claimed by a Dragon. I think I'm going to be up for the rest of the night."

"You *are* tense. Why don't you slip into the hot tub?"

The room had its own hot tub? Of *course,* it did – Dragons didn't rent cheap rooms. "That sounds like a great idea."

"How about that wine you turned down before? Ready for it now?"

"The room came with *wine?*"

"Yes. A very nice pinot noir."

Okay, from now on, the First Flight was making *all* her reservations! "That would be wonderful, thanks."

As she stepped onto the balcony, the stillness of the desert night wrapped her in its embrace. One by one, she slipped her clothes off and placed them, folded, beside the tub. Instinctively, her hand rose to shield her breasts. It felt strange to be naked outside. A little delicious too, in an impish, mischievous way.

Beyond the railing lay nothing except darkness. No other balconies or rooms looked out on hers. Slowly, Savannah lowered her arm. Nothing (except a coyote or two) could see her. On bare feet, she stepped to the tub, savoring the slightly scandalous feel of cool air on her skin.

Steam rose from the hot tub, and she sank, gladly, into its depths. A sigh escaped her as warm water enveloped her poor, tired muscles. Droplets pearled on her fingertips as she pressed a button. With a faint hum, the water bubbled as the tub's jets kicked in.

Currents swirled around her. Under its whispering touch, her skin awoke. Sore muscles relaxed, nerves quivered at the water's caress. One cheeky jet sent a current swirling between her legs and stirred the short hair of her sex. Its sly touch brought a smile to her lips.

"I thought you needed this."

Jordan knelt and set a tray down beside her. Two wine glasses, half full of rich, purple liquid. And beside them, a bowl of…

"Oh, my word! Where did you find chocolate covered strawberries at this hour?"

"In the kitchen. By the wine."

Dragon reservations *forever*. Savannah raised a glass to her lips and sipped. Laced with hints of cherry and cloves, the wine swirled about her tongue. As the bubbling water soothed her body, the pinot's gentle touch calmed her fretting, anxious mind. Tomorrow would bring problems – and she would deal with them. Tonight, the wine promised, there was only peace.

Smiling, Jordan held a strawberry out for her. She nipped

it, her lips brushing playfully against his fingers. "You should join me."

He rose to his feet and turned, as if he planned to change inside. But when he saw the disappointment on her face, his eyes sparkled, and he stepped back in full view. He kicked off his shoes without a thought. Then, he raised his hands.

Slowly, he began to unbutton his shirt. Fingers teased each button apart. The first parted to reveal his throat. The second, the first wisps of chest hair. Savannah felt her breath slow as his hands drifted lower, taunting her with their glacial pace. Now, silk opened to reveal hot, chiseled muscles. Abs, sharp and hard; a flat, taut stomach. When the last button surrendered, he slipped a hand below, down into his pants. Her heart skipped a beat, imagining what treasure it found there. Cloth swelled as he stroked himself. Whispering, with his touch, a promise to his manhood. Rousing it. Calling it.

Then, his hand rose and, with a shrug, he tossed off his shirt. Now, nothing hid him from her eager, hungry eyes. The play of his muscles, shaded lightly by fine, dark curls. The sweep of that taut stomach. The hard curves of his biceps.

Once more, his hand descended – to pop open the button at the top of his pants. Fingers curled around his zipper and tugged it, slowly, *oh so slowly*, down. Red silk jockeys crept into view, and a luscious, delectable swell. Then, he lifted both hands to his stomach and swept them down. Pants fell, in slow motion, across broad, tight thighs and sculpted calves. When they reached his ankles, he kicked them off and stood proudly before her. Only that scrap of silk remained. Beneath it, she saw the bulge of his manhood. Desire made flesh, and growing as he stood, savoring her hunger and admiration.

Then it, too, was swept aside. Jordan stood before her.

Naked. Strong. Masculine perfection. His manhood aroused and ready.

He slipped into the pool beside her, joining her in its hot embrace. Now, it was her turn to offer him fruit, to enjoy the delicate tingle of his lips on her fingers. Together, they sipped their wine and traded offerings of sweet strawberries.

There was no rush, no hurry. No crisis threatened to drag them apart. Left alone, she could savor the languid, delicious details. The way drops of water caught in his chest hair, glittering like tiny diamonds. The hard planes of his leg pressed against hers. How his lips parted in desire as the bubbling water caught her breasts and set them dancing on its tiny waves.

This was what 'forever' would be like with him.

At some point, the last of the strawberries vanished. The wine sat beside them, forgotten, as they turned to other, more delicious desires.

Each other.

Jordan drew her to him. His lips met hers, as she'd longed to have happen. She wrapped her arms around him, erasing the distance between them. As they kissed, hands explored wet skin. His stroked the slick curves of her flank and buttocks. Hers traced the muscles of his back, marveling at the odd, male power of his form. So different from the gentle curves of her own.

Damp hair chafed against her nipples and they stiffened at that touch. Through parted lips, her tongue darted. Tasting his mouth. Teasing him. Urging him to explore hers. Everywhere their bodies touched, wet skin slid smoothly, turning every move into a caress.

When he withdrew at last, deep, ragged breaths shook Savannah's slender form. The slow dance of mouth and hand had fully awoken her desire. Fanning the embers of that slow, delicious burn into something fiercer. A need that could no longer be denied.

Jordan slid from the bench, kneeling in the tub's center. He pulled her to him. Almost weightless in the water's hot embrace, she drifted with ease. His hands caught her, cupping her buttocks, and held her aloft.

Somewhere close, just beneath her parted legs, his cock awaited. If he had taken her then, she would not have complained. Wet, ready, she could have happily surrendered to him and been satisfied.

But satisfaction was not enough for Jordan. Never. Dragons simply did not accept anything less than the best. Not even the fallen ones.

Holding her aloft, he brought her to his waiting mouth. The waters offered her breasts to him and he accepted their gift. A kiss upon her nipple, then another. Hungrier. More insistent. Savannah wrapped her legs around his chest. Not because he needed help holding her. No, for the simple, animal pleasure of feeling the heat of his body pressed against her sex.

Tongue, waves, and lips joined to madden her. Circling her aureoles. Lapping her nipples. Whispering across her breasts. She leaned back, safe in his powerful arms, and let him devour her.

The fire within her blazed. Her legs tightened with each of his caresses, pressing herself against him. Rubbing against the hard lines of his muscles. As her need grew more urgent, she writhed, her body silently begging him for completion.

A demand he was eager to fulfill.

He lowered her slowly. Body sinking through the water, she felt the tip of his cock nuzzle between her legs. That touch, that promise, wrenched a moan of need from her. Jordan kissed her reverently, as if he could taste her desire.

Then, he settled her down upon himself. His cock, thick and hard, slipped inside her.

With a gasp of pleasure, she clung to him. Arms wrapped around his shoulders. Legs curled about his hips, drawing him deep within her. For a moment, she held him, with arms and legs, with her body, reveling in the sheer, delirious bliss of feeling him inside her. Of being filled and completed.

Then, Jordan took her.

His hips surged, pushing her up. Water splashed over her breasts, his cock thrusting into her. Before she could slip free, he pulled her down again. Water claimed her and his manhood drove, once more, into her hidden depths.

Savannah gasped with the sudden, delightful shock of it. Once more, he raised her and this time, she joined him. Legs tightening, squeezing. Taking *him*, claiming *him*.

Never had she felt such power, such control. She rode him, each thrust in time with her rhythms, her desires. Beneath her, Jordan moaned, the master now begging *her* for release. Rocking, squeezing, she teased his manhood. Felt it swell, heard his cries of need and longing.

Until, at last, he surged up, meeting her as she took him. With a groan, he came, filling her with his seed. Fed by his release, her own passion crested. Ecstasy washed over her. Her legs closed around him, holding him tight. Savoring that orgasm, as if she could make it last forever.

With a soft sigh, she released him. Drifting back into the water's arms. Watching the pleasure, the fulfillment, on his face.

And when, some minutes later, they abandoned the tub and their wine, Savannah found that, yes, she could finally sleep. Curled in his arms, at last, she surrendered to her dreams.

Whatever the morning brought, they would face it together.

CHAPTER 15

Morning brought breakfast in bed. Belgian waffles piled high with berries and whipped cream. A dark, bitter coffee that perked Savannah up and got her ready to face the day. Then, a shower – shared, for the first time in her life. Soap, warm water, and the even hotter presence of Jordan's taut, hard body. Afterward, they made love again. Another gentle union, with plenty of time to cuddle and explore. A shadow lay over their love making. Her lover held tight to every moment, savoring it, as if he thought this might be their last time together.

It might be. She couldn't deny the possibility that today, he might be condemned to death.

She couldn't believe it, either. Not when Finn Donnelly let them spend the night in peace. That gesture, so welcome, was a great act of faith.

He gave them most of the morning too, to dawdle in the hot tub and fill the time with small talk. Not until a half hour before noon did the Dragon appear and burst the bubble of peace they'd built.

Back to the ranch house on the edge of town.

The crowd was much smaller this time. No Wolf Packs milled in the yard, fighting off boredom with mid-morning chaos. Even the judges had changed. Witch Queen LePierre was there. Of course. Savannah wouldn't have been shocked if the woman had camped out all night, determined not to miss a chance to condemn Jordan. Beside her sat Rex Fairburn and Griffin Davis, men she hoped would support her. None of the male Wolf Alphas had come. Instead, Aaron King's daughter, Lily, showed up with her brother, Lucas.

Almost late. They stumbled through the door just behind Savannah, visibly hung over.

LePierre turned a disapproving stare upon them. "Ms. King, where is your father and the other Wolves?"

"Hell of a party last night. Dad's face-down in a puddle of his own vomit," Lily announced cheerfully. "Don't worry. I rolled him over. He won't drown."

"I assume he will not attend these proceedings either?" The Hare couldn't keep the disgust off her face.

Lily ignored it. "Nope."

"Well, we will do without him, then. As the female Alpha of your Pack, I assume you will vote in his stead?"

"Yep."

"And your brother votes for…?"

"Nobody. He's a loser!" She grinned with glee as Lucas flipped her the bird.

"Hey, unlike you, this 'loser' got invited by the First Flight." The Wolf added another middle finger to his salute, and his sister laughed.

The Witch Queen ignored their antics and play-fight. "Mr. Donnelly, may I ask the reason for that invitation?"

"It'll come up later, after the trial."

The last person to enter was SueSue Mint. She slipped through the door and slunk along the wall. Rats did that when they didn't feel safe, much like true rodents. Passing

Jordan, the old woman paused. "Thanks for killing that SOB Manning. Wish you could have killed him slower."

"You're welcome." Jordan bowed his head, offering the Rat a courtesy few Shifters showed her Kind. "I understand your desire for vengeance, but Savannah's safety was my greatest concern."

"As it should be." Life hadn't been kind to SueSue; it rarely was to Rats. Yet, suffering had given her a strength and endurance as great as any Dragon's. "The living always matter more than the dead."

Then, she scurried past and pulled a chair close to Rex Fairburn's side. The one Shifter in this room she trusted fully.

Ever the proper lady, LePierre nodded at the other judges. "Unless there are objections, I suggest we vote immediately. There's no point wasting more time."

No point 'wasting' time – to save a man's life? Savannah's eyes flashed with outrage. "I object!"

"I remind you, Kin-woman, that you don't have a vote."

Oh no, that arrogant rabbit was *not* going to silence her! Hands balled into fists, Savannah stormed over to the Hare. LePierre shied away, her nose wrinkling as if a skunk had charged her. "I don't care if–"

"Ladies!" Finn Donnelly's booming voice froze them both. "I *do* have a vote, and I've got something to add. Last night, Briggs and I discovered that Jordan Beaumont isn't a Worm. He's a, uh, Dragon-y kind of Wormy thing with freaky half-wings."

Silence. All the judges peered at him in confusion.

Briggs cleared his throat. "I believe what the emissary of the First Flight means is that Mr. Beaumont's Dragon soul has begun to heal itself."

"Is that possible?" LePierre scoffed. "Can a Worm actually become a Dragon once more?"

"Dunno," Donnelly admitted. "Guess we're going to find out."

"Unless he is condemned," the Hare reminded him. "Do you have any other news?"

"Yep. Mr. Beaumont has Claimed a Mate. Her." The Dragon pointed at Savannah.

Gasps rang out. Around the room, Shifters recoiled. Lips pinched, chin raised, Savannah met their gazes without flinching. Let them sneer. Let them stare. She didn't care. The more polite ones, like Rex Fairburn, tried to hide their shock. Yet, even SueSue seemed startled that a woman could love a Worm.

Not everyone in the room was as polite as them, however. Danielle LePierre made no effort to hide her revulsion. Disgust twisted her delicate face into a mask of horror. "You allowed a Worm to Claim you?" she murmured. As if that was the sickest, most depraved thing she'd ever heard.

Savannah Dare was a calm person, by necessity. Excitable spies didn't last long. But at the sight of that disgust, that arrogant loathing... something inside her snapped. Rage – towering, red, and seething – rose within her. Her hand balled into a fist and she swung it with all her might at the Hare's smug, conceited face.

Lily, who sat beside her, moved with lightning speed. Before the blow connected, she caught Savannah's hand in a shockingly strong grip. One that stopped the swing an inch in front of the Hare's nose. LePierre gave a startled squeak as the Wolf said, "Sorry. Can't let you do that."

Savannah shot Lily a disappointed glare. A Wolf? Of all people, a *Wolf* wouldn't let her punch this woman in the face?

One hand held her wrist in an iron grip. With the other, Lily pried her fingers apart. "You got your thumb inside your fingers. You'll break it if you slug someone that way. Keep it on the outside. Like this." Gently, she tugged Savannah's thumb up, then wrapped her fingers into a fist once more, thumb curled on the outside. "There you are. Good to go."

Lily released her hand and stepped back, face bright with joyous expectation.

LePierre's brief flash of fear had already died, killed by annoyance. "What are you blathering about, Ms. King?"

Savannah punched her in the face. Hard.

And, to Lily's credit, she did *not* break her thumb. However, a satisfying burst of blood exploded from the Hare's nose, and she shrieked in pain and shock.

That wail sent the Wolf howling with glee. "And Dad said trials were boring!"

"Lily!" Briggs groaned, appalled (once more) by his Wolf Mate.

"What? Bunny-girl had it coming."

Hand clamped over her streaming nose, Danielle LePierre bolted from the room. Savannah glared after her until she scrambled out the door, then stalked back and took her seat next to her shocked Mate.

Only Lily laughed out loud – but Griffin and SueSue fought to keep a straight face.

Donnelly, however, sighed dramatically. "And, once again, we've lost our quorum."

The Chimera leaned forward and lowered his voice to a conspiratorial stage whisper. "Hey, I've got an idea. Why don't the rest of us vote without her? I'm sure Danielle won't mind. I mean, yesterday, she insisted nobody but Dragons really ought to get a say. So, we're down one Hare? Who cares?"

"Griffin," Donnelly groaned.

"I'll start. Mate and a soul make all the difference in the world to me. I say give Nemo... er, Beaumont, another chance."

As soon as the Chimera cast his vote, SueSue added her own. "He killed Manning. I say he lives."

"SueSue," Rex groaned, "that's not sensible."

"You got your reasons, Bear. I got mine." The Rat folded her arms across her chest.

"Fairburn?" Donnelly prompted.

The Bear shrugged. "A Mate matters. If somebody could love him, he's worth a shot."

"I agree." Briggs nodded at his Mate. "What about you, Lily?"

"He's done nothing to me. I say he lives. And wipe that look off your face, Casey, or I will come over there and slap it off. It's like the Rat said: I don't have to defend my reasons."

Which left only the First Flight. "I vote in favor too. So, I guess it doesn't matter that the Witch Queen left. She's either with us, or out-voted."

Jordan remained impassive as his fate was decided. Neither relief nor fear troubled his handsome face. Only Savannah, seated by his side, heard a soft inhale. The sole clue of how relieved he was.

Unlike him, she felt no urge to hide her feelings. Eyes closed to fight back tears, she lifted his hand to her lips and kissed his fingers. The man she loved, the man she dared to redeem, would not be torn from her. Not today.

A tender moment – that lasted only a second before Lily said, "Where's the beer?"

Everyone turned to the Wolf. "What beer?" her Mate asked.

"This is a trial! How can you not have beer?" Savannah bit back a smile. The Wolf loved playing the buffoon, but she was a sharp, sharp woman. "Okay, from now on, I organize all trials. That way, we have something to drink to celebrate our decisions."

Her joke did its job: The trial's icy formality finally shattered. Freed from it, people began to chat and mingle. A couple, like Griffin and Rex, even came over to shake Jordan's hand.

Savannah stayed close by his side. Offering him the comfort, the wordless support, of her presence. This was where his healing would begin. Among his people, other Shifters. With small talk and teasing. Normal things that regular people did every day. Things that had grown completely alien to the Worm over the long centuries.

But as the gathering began to dissolve, Donnelly cleared his throat and shot Lily a pointed stare. "So, before people head out on beer runs, there's one more thing I want to try. Lucas, you have the Aegis, yes?"

"Yeah." Lily's brother opened his denim jacket and lifted his shirt – to reveal a bag strapped across his chest. "I'm not losing this thing again." From it, he withdrew a plate-sized 'shield' of white leather.

Savannah's heart skipped a beat. The Aegis. The key to locking the demon lord Nemagorix out of this world. (*If anyone could figure out how to use it…*)

Four images lined its edges, drawn in black ink. A horned Dragon, a Wolf, a Bear, and a winged lion, which must be Griffin's Chimera. A blank patch of leather left room for a fifth.

Donnelly turned to face Jordan. "Last night, our Not-Quite-A-Worm tried to fly."

"Unsuccessfully," her lover admitted.

"True. Because your wings are damaged. They're not real wings, they're bones and tatters."

"Holy hell." Rex Fairburn's jaw dropped. "You think he's…"

"I do." Turning to Savannah and Jordan, Donnelly grew somber. "We know that, in order to defend this world, the

Aegis needs to bond to five Shifters. So far, it's chosen Casey Briggs, Lucas Clay, Rex Fairburn, and Griffin Davis."

Dragon, Wolf, Bear, and Chimera. That explained the ink figures!

"Fairburn found an ancient drawing that revealed all five Shifters. The one we're missing is a skeletal creature with bone wings. We had *no* idea what that might be… until last night, when we saw Beaumont's messed up Dragon."

They thought her Mate might be the last Shifter of the Aegis?

Pride filled her, setting her face alight with joy. *Her* Mate! *Her* Dragon! (And yes, that's what he was: A Dragon. Injured, weighed down by years of despair… but a Dragon's heart still beat within his chest. She would never think of him as a 'Worm' again. Nothing was further from the truth!)

Jordan paled as the full impact of Donnelly's words hit him. "You believe that the Aegis might choose… me?"

"Only one way to find out. Lucas?"

The young Wolf stepped forward and held out the little shield.

A tremor shook Jordan's hand as he reached for it – the tiniest crack in the flawless self-control he prided himself in. Her Mate paused, clenched his fist tightly, until that faint weakness passed. He didn't open his hand again until he was once more his own master.

Dazed and proud, he laid a finger on the Aegis.

Nothing happened.

Around the circle, faces fell. "Well, dammit," Donnelly muttered. "I thought I had it all figured out."

Savannah's heart fell as well… then broke when she saw the mask of icy indifference that Jordan quickly donned.

How much worse was this for him? To dare to hope that, finally, after so many long years, he meant something? That he could do good, a noble deed to lighten the debt of sin his soul bore? One second of hope, one moment to dream… and then, reality came crashing back. He was a Worm. Unclean. Unworthy of a relic like the Aegis.

Those thoughts, so harsh, so unloving, shocked her. Anger burned away her disappointment; anger at herself.

I need to be strong enough to hope for both of us.

"It's okay." She slid close to him, pressing against him and slipping an arm around his waist. "It doesn't matter."

Stiff, unyielding, Jordan rejected the comfort she offered. "I'm not surprised."

"There's no shame in having the Aegis thumb its nose at you," Donnelly insisted. "Thing didn't have any use for me either."

The Dragon didn't understand. He couldn't. He wasn't a Worm. He didn't realize that hope was a double-edged blade, as dangerous as it was necessary.

Savannah did. "You can't blame yourself. This doesn't say anything about you."

"Oh, I don't think it does, don't worry." Those were the words she longed to hear. They fell from his lips so easily, so glibly, however, that she couldn't believe them. "In fact, I haven't given up yet."

That did cheer her. Even more when he turned to the Dragons and said, "May I ask a great favor of you? Will you leave me here along with the Aegis and my Mate? I think I may know a way to get this relic to change its opinion about me."

"I would prefer that one of us Dragons stayed here as well. I'm willing to give you a second shot, buddy – but that doesn't mean I trust you with the Aegis."

"There is something I need to do which I cannot in the presence of another."

No one except her? What…? Oh!

Savannah blushed. He wanted to make love? Perhaps that *would* prove to the Aegis that he had changed.

Donnelly's mind followed the exact same path as hers. "Oh. Er, gotcha. Well, we can give you some space. Though – fair warning – we'll be right outside, watching. Don't try to leave this house with the Aegis."

"Of course not," Jordan promised.

The other Shifters filed out. Some, like Casey Briggs, scrupulously polite. Others, like his Mate Lily, on the verge of teasing. Briggs dragged her outside before she could do something obnoxious like wolf-whistle.

Which left Savannah and her own Mate, alone.

CHAPTER 16

*E*ven though they were lovers and Mates, the idea of sex on demand wasn't exactly romantic. Especially since Savannah could still hear people outside. Lily's high laugh cut through the walls with a special ease.

Not sexy. Not sexy at all.

"Maybe we should move into the bedroom? Away from the front door?"

Jordan stared at the Aegis, as if mesmerized. He didn't even seem to hear her question.

"Jordan?"

"Hmm?"

"The bedroom?"

"Oh." Like a man waking from a deep sleep, he shook his head. "No, this will do fine."

On *that* sofa? Oh, it was clean and nice, all right. And about a foot and a half wide. Surely, he wasn't suggesting they make love on the floor? Rug or no, that was *not* comfortable!

"I'd prefer a bed."

Jordan gave a tired, half-hearted chuckle. "Actually, I didn't ask you to stay because I wanted to make love. There's something I need to say."

Thank goodness! Close outside, a motorcycle roared once and died. Trying to get in the mood with *that* going on was a lost cause!

"Okay. What is it?" She drifted to the couch (a fine place to sit – just not to make love!).

Jordan didn't follow her. Grief lined his handsome face as he stood, Aegis in hand. His was the visage of a man condemned to death – not one who'd just been freed.

"I want you to know that I love you."

Those words should have thrilled her soul. Instead, they cast a chill across her heart, for no joy warmed them. His confession of love was as sad, as cold, as a funeral eulogy. "Jordan, what's wrong?"

"Nothing."

Oh, no, that was *not* true!

With a sad smile, he stepped to her side and placed a hand on her elbow. "I just want you to know that you saved me. You gave me hope when I despaired. You believed in me when no one else would. Because of you, I literally found my soul again."

Why did that sound more like a suicide note than words of love? "You know this is only the beginning, right? You'll heal. You'll get better. I'll stay with you while you do too because I… I love you too."

That melancholy smile grew strained. "Good. Now, would you leave me, please?"

Alone? With the Aegis? "Why?"

"I need to focus. There was a clue in the Fangs' research, one I believe may be a hint on how I can bind myself to the Aegis?"

Really? She didn't remember that... or did she? Something woke at the back of Savannah's mind. Some odd fact, some unpleasant idea she hadn't believed. "How?"

"Let me just try, all right?"

"No, tell me what you're going to do. I don't recall any–"

"Savannah?" He cupped her chin and laid a thumb gently against her lips. "Do you trust me?"

"...yes..." Right now, that almost felt like a lie.

"Then, please, give me five minutes alone."

How could she refuse? If she denied him this, she proved she didn't trust him. Could any love survive that?

No. Words and deeds *had* to be one. Rising onto her tiptoes, she planted a kiss on his lips. "You know I love you, right?"

"I do. I just need you to trust me too."

"Okay."

Feeling like it was the worst mistake of her life, she left him.

The moment the front door clicked closed behind her, Lily trotted over. "No way! That was like three minutes! Nobody could get it on in–"

"Lily!" her Mate hissed. "Manners, please, I beg you!"

A blush crept across Savannah's cheeks at the Wolf's impudent question. "He just wanted to talk to me."

"Uh huh. And...?"

"And nothing."

"Then you left him alone in there with the Aegis? Why?"

That was just damned impertinent! "Because I trust him!" she snapped at the rude woman.

Unfortunately, to Wolves, challenges were a way of life. Lily didn't take the hint. Just wrinkled her nose and forged on. "You trusted a man to think by himself? Girlfriend, that is the dumbest thing any woman can do!" Behind her, Briggs fluffed with indignation. Lily, however, was on a roll. "This speech he gave you – was it weird?"

"No. Well…" She remembered his expression as they parted. Grieving, sad. Completely at odds with his loving words. "Kind of…"

The Wolf began to bounce from one foot to the other. "I knew it. Get back in there! Guys *always* give weird speeches right before they do stupid ass stuff!"

Alarms were ringing in Savannah's mind. Something about that Fang record she couldn't quite remember… the somber tone of Jordan's words – like he was saying goodbye. But… "He begged me to trust him!"

"Oooh, Kiss of Death! Red flag! He's up to shit!" Lily shrieked.

She should have laughed or slapped the annoying woman. Instead, all her fears came rushing back, crashing down on her with the force of an avalanche. More than an intuition, Savannah knew – with no doubt or question – that something was wrong.

Was this what a Dragon felt when his Mate's life was in danger? Adrenaline flashed through her and drove her, sprinting, back into the house. Like a dog chasing a car, Lily bolted after her.

"Jordan!"

Savannah burst in on a scene so strange that, at first, her mind could make no sense of it.

Frozen with shock, Jordan stood where she'd left him. The Aegis lay on the ground at his feet. And his hands…

His hands were Dragon claws. Scaled. Tipped with deadly talons. One lay on his cheek, as if he'd just slapped himself.

"Savannah! What…?"

Why did his fingers curl so? Why did shame paint his cheeks a brilliant red?

Then it came back to her. That one, critical fact that had slipped her mind. According to the Fangs' reports, Nemagorix insisted that the last person the Aegis chose needed to die.

He meant to kill himself. To wake the shield's protections with his life's blood.

Her shock betrayed her; Jordan saw it and knew the game was up. "I'm sorry. If there were any other way…" Lethal talons dropped to his throat.

Half a room lay between them. She could never cross it in time.

But Lily stood at her elbow. With a gun holstered at her side. In a blur of movement, Savannah grabbed it – and raised the muzzle to her own temple. "Stop or I'll shoot!"

People froze, both inside and outside the door. "Whoa, that's a new one," Lily muttered as she edged away, hands held up in surrender.

"Savannah, put that gun down, now!" Jordan roared.

"No! I love you and I'm staying with you, in this world or the next. If you die, I die!" A lie would never fool a Mate; she meant what she said. Yet, she prayed his Dragon would not see through a bluff. That, as it had in their dreams, it would abandon its foolishness to save her.

Donnelly inched forward carefully. "Ms. Dare, why is anybody dying? Beaumont? What the hell is going on?"

"He's going to tear his own throat out!" Savannah snapped. "Dragon claws are the only thing tough enough to tear through a Dragon's own scales!"

Jordan didn't contradict her. "Information the Fangs uncovered suggested that the last spot on the Aegis would be filled by a dead man."

"Nemagorix said that," Griffin admitted. "That someone needed to die."

"Since when do we do what demons tell us?" she growled.

Jordan winced, as if she'd kicked him in the shin. But, to her relief, he lowered his hand, the first hint of doubt darkening his face. "Do you have *any* other evidence? *Any* reason to believe that a demon lord would just blurt out the key to its own defeat?"

No one offered any. Jordan actually had the grace to shuffle his feet. "I admit, it sounds foolish when you put it like that..."

"That's because it *is* foolish! Idiotic! The stupidest thing I've ever heard!" she screamed.

"Okay, okay. Calm down." Claws shrank into fingers as he held his hands out. One tiny drop of blood clung to his fingertip and dripped to the floor. "I won't hurt myself. I promise. Now, you've got to put that gun down before you kill yourself."

"Don't worry!" Lily chirped. "She's fine. I didn't want to ruin your moment, girl, but you forgot to click the safety off."

"That was deliberate. Last thing this day needs is for me to accidentally blow my brains out."

The Wolf snickered, an unladylike, whiffling snort that was contagious as hell. To Jordan's outrage, Savannah started to giggle. The other woman joined her, and suddenly, both of them howled with laughter.

"You really were going to kill yourself though!" the Worm protested. "I could tell!"

"Well, sure, but..." The rest of her words got lost in chuckles of pure relief.

Jordan rushed over and pushed the gun aside. As the others crowded into the room, he pulled her into his arms. "Don't ever do that. Don't *ever* threaten to kill yourself!"

"You did it first!" she sniffed back.

Lily stepped around them to retrieve her gun. "Yeah, kick his ass," she muttered. "He's got it coming."

The rest of the Shifters wandered in, still uneasy. "Okay,"

Donnelly sighed, "are we officially back to the 'No One Dies Today' plan?"

"We are," a chastised Jordan promised.

Lucas, the Aegis' guardian, retrieved the little shield – then frowned and held it up for all to see. "Uh, guys? Check this out."

A fifth figure filled the final gap. A skeletal Dragon – drawn in blood, not ink.

The drop of blood that had fallen from Jordan's fingertip.

"What the hell?" Donnelly's wonder was reflected on the faces of the other Shifters.

Yet, to Savannah, it made sense. "The best lies have a kernel of truth in their hearts. Maybe you didn't need to die – but you had to be willing to sacrifice yourself." Swelling with pride, she snuggled against him, reveling in his dazed, delighted smile.

The Aegis had chosen him.

Jordan Beaumont was now officially one of the 'good guys.'

A long and painful road lay ahead of him. No doubt, there were tons of terrible sins for which he needed to atone.

But she would be there, by his side. Lending him her strength when his failed.

It was beautiful, the proudest moment of her life.

Until three gasps of horror shattered it.

Donnelly, Griffin, and Lucas all staggered, shock flashing across their faces.

"I have to go!" The Dragon spun toward the door – and collided with the Wolf and Chimera.

"Maddie!" Griffin gasped. Wings were already sprouting from his shoulders, as if his soul – a winged golden lion – planned to burst through the wall.

"Ash is in trouble!" Lucas howled. Fur had burst out along his face and arms, like a werewolf from some old movie.

Before the three men could go spilling out into the desert, Briggs bellowed, "HOLD! Think, fools! You cannot simply run off to them. They are not near."

The urge to defend a Mate was the strongest force a Shifter could know. Briggs' advice was good – but almost impossible for them to heed. Lucas Shifted fully, snarling with rage at the horned Dragon. Donnelly and Griffin managed to hold themselves back. Barely.

Savannah's heart raced. She and Lily – two other Mates – were all right. The Wolf Princess turned to Rex. "Omega okay?"

The name confused her, but not the Bear. "Paige is fine."

Oh, right. 'Omega' was a Wolf nickname for the smallest member of the Pack. Lily must be a friend of the Bear's Mate.

Faced with chaos and confusion, Jordan's natural urge to lead came to the fore. "You three. Where are your Mates? We need to figure out what could threaten all of them at once."

Three Shifters spun and pointed in the same direction: northwest.

"Are they at Stillwater?"

Stillwater. The name sent a chill down Savannah's spine. That was the remote Navajo village which guarded the main gate to the realm of the demon lord Nemagorix.

Men (and Wolf) nodded. Briggs swore softly. "Too far. I will get a helicopter for us. That will be quicker."

"Any phones there?" Jordan asked. "Some way to get in touch?"

Briggs shook his head.

Then they would fly in blind. Because nothing would keep three Shifters away when their Mates were in danger.

Perhaps the Fangs (or their secret Darkborn masters) had assaulted the gate. Savannah almost hoped that was true, because the alternative was worse: That, somehow, Nemagorix knew when the Aegis chose Jordan. The demon could sense its bane, the only thing that could bind it, was whole once more.

If that was true, the final battle had just begun.

CHAPTER 17

Five seats. Eight people. That was the best helicopter Briggs could find on short notice.

Jordan and the two Dragons crouched in the middle of the floor. They were the strongest Shifters; if they got tossed about, it wouldn't hurt them. That left the seats (and seat belts) to the more 'delicate' people. Wolves, Chimera, Bear…

And Savannah. Jordan glared at her, furious that she was even there.

"Stop it," she scowled back, completely impervious to his most domineering glower.

"You should have stayed in Sedona. You're going to distract me."

"Then *you* need to control *your* self."

"There's nothing you can do. You're not even a Shifter."

The moment those words slipped from his lips, he hated himself. That was the chink in Savannah's armor, the 'flaw' that made her doubt herself. How could he attack her in such an underhanded way?

I must. I need to keep her safe – even if it means hurting her.

Unfortunately, not even a low blow helped his case.

Breaking free of Todd Manning had strengthened her confidence. "Jordan, I'm a trained agent. I'll be fine."

"Have you had martial arts or self-defense training?"

"I don't plan on running up to any demons and punching them in the nose." Bulky body armor swathed her graceful form and she patted the gun holstered by her side. "I'll keep my distance and use this."

His fear, his agony, must have shown on his face because, for a moment, her indignation faded. She reached out and gave his hand a reassuring squeeze. "It will be okay. I'll help where I can, but trust me, I'm not going to barge into the middle of things. I know my limits."

Hard as it was, he would have to trust her. To be honest, he'd lost this battle the moment the helicopter took off. With three Mates in danger, they were *not* turning around. Dumping Savannah in the middle of the desert wasn't an option either.

No, she was going with him, into the storm.

Literally.

An enormous thunder cloud towered in the distance. Black clouds etched by flashes of lightning rose thousands of feet into the air. Somewhere beneath it lay Stillwater, a handful of trailers and stone huts miles from any paved road.

Nemagorix was there too. In the heart of that maelstrom.

Beads of sweat ran down their pilot's face. He served the Flight of the Snows, but the man wasn't a soldier. On a normal workday, he simply whisked Dragons from one private airport to another. Flying straight into the mouth of a storm wasn't part of his job description. "How close is this town to that thing?"

"At its base," Briggs warned. "Perhaps even inside its edge."

"I can't fly into that."

"I understand. Get us as close as you can."

Pressed against Savannah's legs, Jordan turned his thoughts to their problem. What would they face in Stillwater?

Darkborn, certainly. Nemagorix had nearly slipped its bonds a couple weeks ago. That attack unleashed a slew of possessing spirits. Deranged elementals were another threat, though he hoped that most of them had been destroyed during the last assault. Other vile creatures dwelled in Nemagorix's realm. In an all-out attack, they might pour into this world too.

A depressing thought. But was it all they needed to worry about?

No. Better than any other Shifter, Jordan knew that. The Fangs had done their best to weed the Darkborn out of their ranks – but that job was far from done.

If there's a compromised cell nearby, we could be facing both Nemagorix and the Fangs of Apophis.

So, what was close? He mourned his laptop, left back at the resort. Without it, he struggled to remember the locations of the Fang enclaves in the south-west. Death Valley had been purged… it should be clean. Dry Lake could be a threat, except it was too far away. Blanding?

Blanding was a problem. It housed a rapid response team – and had no review in the last year, as far as he knew. Worse, that team was expected to face attacks from the Flight of the Snows. Which meant it was prepared to take on Dragons.

A former Fang, Jordan knew exactly what that meant.

"Pilot. Keep an eye out for other helicopters," he called out, raising his voice to be heard above the rotors' whine.

His words roused Donnelly from his brooding for one moment. "Fangs?"

"Yes. The Blanding outpost isn't far. They're equipped with a half dozen choppers with air-to-air missiles. They can fly circles around a little recreational copter like this one."

"And blow it to shrapnel. Thanks for the warning," the Dragon replied.

Their pilot didn't share his appreciation. Sweat went from a trickle to a steady stream down his cheeks. Despite his fear, though, he wasn't the one who spotted the attack when it came.

Jordan felt it, a flash of fear that snapped him into battle readiness.

Our Mate... danger...

Briggs jolted to his feet at the same moment. "Incoming!" Jordan bawled. Anger seethed within him, a powerless fury that was alien to him. There was nothing he could do to protect his Mate. If this helicopter was shot out of the sky, he might survive.

Savannah would not. Not even if he tried to shield her with his own body.

He was failing her.

Because I drove my Dragon mad. Because I let myself become so corrupt that it chewed its wings off.

But Donnelly and Briggs possessed what he lacked. At his cry, the big Dragon yanked open the helicopter door. Wind whipped violently around him. "We'll take care of the Fangs," he shouted. "Meet you in town."

With that, the two men threw themselves into the air. Falling, falling... then, in a burst of light and magic, they Shifted. Two Dragons rose into the air, black and white. Together, they surged ahead as the helicopter slowed.

Just in time. Four choppers streaked up from the ground. Four sets of missiles fired.

"Down!" Jordan roared at the pilot. "Get us lower!"

Faster than the eye could follow, those deadly missiles shot toward them. Honing in on their defenseless aircraft...

Until two enormous gouts of fire flashed through the air, weaving a molten shield. The missiles slammed into it and exploded.

The blast nearly flipped their little chopper. Jordan went sailing across the floor as their pilot screamed in terror. His hand flailed out and caught the edge of Savannah's chair in a death grip, just before he went sailing out the open door.

Let's not *test whether Worms are as tough as Dragons...*

Righting at last, the chopper plunged toward the ground. Overhead, blasts of fire and machine guns rang out. Another explosion, and suddenly, burning shrapnel and bits of twisted metal rained past them.

Direct hit on one of our enemies.

And here he sat. Useless. Relying on a mortal pilot to save his Mate.

He should be out there with Briggs and Donnelly. Destroying his enemies. Lord of the air, master of the skies.

A *Dragon.*

But he wasn't. He was a Worm, a wing-less *thing* that couldn't shield his Mate from–

Soft yet strong, Savannah's hand squeezed his shoulder. "Stop it. You're beating yourself up again. I can see it on your face."

They nearly got blown out of the sky… and she wanted to comfort him?

Of course, she does. She's my Mate.

She was but she was also Bear Kin, and Bears didn't baby their loved ones. They were as tough, and as honest, as they needed to be. "It took you centuries to dig this hole, Jordan. Don't expect to hop out of it with one good day. Just keep trying. You'll get there."

Down they dropped, as war raged overhead. Their pilot skimmed low across the ground, cacti and rocks whipping past.

He *could* shield Savannah if they crashed. That sense of helplessness, so alien and terrible, receded. As it did, something inside him calmed.

My Dragon. Or what's left of it.

How many years had it been since it last spoke to him? Long enough that he thought it dead.

I've forgotten what it's like to be a true Shifter. To have a second spirit, another soul, joined to you.

Savannah was right. It would take time to climb out of the hole he'd dug.

Ahead, stony pillars jutted high into the sky. Stillwater, a tiny collection of huts and trailers, lay at their base. Somewhere, a small path wove through those rock walls into the tiny dell they hid in. A clearing that held the pond that gave Stillwater its name.

And the gate to Nemagorix's prison.

No rain fell from the storm that boiled above them, but a gloom crept over the land as they passed under its shadow, riven only by the bolts of lightning that streaked across the sky. Gusts slammed the chopper, tossing it about like a toy plane.

"I've got to land!" the pilot shrieked.

"Do so then!" Jordan shouted back.

A half mile to the town, he stole a quick glance at Savannah, who fidgeted with her body armor. He and the other Shifters could cross that distance with ease. But her? In armor she'd never worn? A half mile ought to slow her down nicely.

Good. Anything to keep her safe. Even leaving her behind was fine by him.

With a jolt, the helicopter scraped to a halt. The moment it touched ground, Shifters tore free of their seat belts, spilling out into the desert and Shifting.

"Let's clear the village first," Jordan began. "The five of us..."

Griffin Shifted into a hawk and flew off without even bothering to hear the rest.

"Guess that makes four of us," he muttered. Not that any of them could blame the Chimera. His Mate was somewhere in that chaos, in mortal danger. Frankly, Jordan was amazed that Lucas was keeping his shit together.

Maybe his Mate isn't in as much danger as Griffin's...

"Let's go."

Once more, he called to his Shifter soul... and it answered. Black scales wrapped his body in almost impenetrable armor. Lethal claws and fangs appeared, ready to shred his enemies. Perhaps it was his imagination, but his wings seemed stronger, less tattered.

Not strong enough to fly, however. Jordan tucked them tight against his flanks and led the charge on Stillwater.

Two Wolves streaked through the scrub to his right. Fairburn, a great Kodiak, charged with shocking speed on his left. Given how large Bears were, it was easy to forget they could sprint faster than a horse.

But the possessed Fangs in town only had one target: Jordan. The Worm. Even a fallen Dragon was a foe few mortals (or Shifters) dared to face. Rifle bullets hit first, from snipers hiding somewhere in the hills. They pinged harmlessly off the scales around his eyes. Lily and Lucas split off from the main charge, hunting the shooters. One bullet hit his eye directly. It stung – like getting snapped by a rubber band. At this distance, though, even his eyes were too tough for their weapons. Jordan ignored them. Let the Wolves handle that threat.

Somewhere far behind them, Savannah ran as fast as she could. His Worm... no, his crippled *Dragon*... gave no warnings for her safety. She was far enough back that she faced no danger.

Just as he'd hoped.

Nearer to town, the first true threat was revealed: A machine gun nest. A hail of armor-piercing bullets sprayed across the desert. Fairburn peeled off, forcing the Fangs to choose one target. Him, or the Bear.

All of them chose him, of course. A mercenary stood a chance against a Bear that closed in on him. A Worm? None. Sharp stings raked across his body as the bullets hit him. They hurt – but he welcomed that pain. It was clean, burning away his self-doubt and guilt. The past no longer mattered. Jordan was here, now, fighting the good fight. Protecting his Mate.

Being a Dragon, not a Worm.

No lesser pain, no mere bullets, could stop him.

One man stepped up near the machine gun and raised a long, heavy tube to his shoulder. Details blurred at this distance, but Jordan recognized it at once.

A T4 rocket. Strong enough to take out tanks.

Or Dragons.

His human mind screamed to dodge. But, for once, he wasn't the master of his own body. He had summoned his Dragon, and it had answered. Jordan Beaumont might fear mortal weapons. His Dragon, however, trusted its own strength. It, not some human with a big stick, reigned supreme in battle.

And so, it charged straight on, ignoring Jordan as he fought to seize control. When the missile flew toward him, it opened its jaws wide and breathed.

If he'd truly been a Dragon, that would have sent a wave of fiery death washing over his foes. They and their impudent weapon would be incinerated. But Worms couldn't breathe. Fire, like air, was denied them. Jordan's last thought was a silent, bitter laugh at the foolishness of his Dragon.

Until a small puff of flame hiccupped out of his maw. Not the great, lethal stream of a full Dragon – but enough to detonate the missile in front of his face.

The blast, though, hit him like a freight truck. With a world-ending roar, it flipped him backward. He was spinning, flailing... and slammed into the ground hard enough to knock the wind out of him.

Not hard enough to stop him. Jordan rose heavily and shook his head as bullets continued to rain down on him. Once more, he staggered forward, growing faster, steadier, as he ran.

Any sane man would flee him. Possessed by the Darkborn, the Fangs didn't have that option. They stood and fought... and died. There was no mercy he could show them. As long as its host lived, a Darkborn could remain in this world – and seek to possess another creature.

Even one as powerful as a Dragon.

So, Jordan killed them all. They died beneath his claws, his fangs, and vicious lashes of a tail which could shatter every bone in a man's body. Dimly, he saw Fairburn fighting, no more gentle than he.

Seconds later, the lopsided battle was over. With snipers dispatched, Lucas and Lily galloped up. Briggs and Donnelly dropped from the sky to join them. Only Griffin was gone, seeking his Mate.

Even poor Savannah staggered into camp, out of breath and too late to fight. He prayed she'd forgive him when this was all done.

Though it's an important lesson for her. She needs to understand that – physically – we are not equal.

Around them, nothing moved. There was no sign of the town's inhabitants or any of the missing Mates.

But no Shifter, neither Wolf nor Dragon, needed a clue to find his woman. Lucas shot off like a furry rocket, tearing through the little hamlet. Out by an old stone wall, he began to dig like a frantic dog. Donnelly Shifted and charged over as well, the others in tow.

One sharp bark from Lucas, and suddenly, the ground rose into the air.

No, not the ground. A sand-covered trap door leading down into some covered pit.

From beneath it, a pretty, round-faced woman peered out. "L-lucas? Is that you?"

With a yip of pure joy, the Wolf began to lick her face.

Ash Anderson. Jordan smiled at the laughing woman. Lucas' Mate.

When she tossed the door aside, two dozen people staggered out of that cramped hidey hole. Most were the town's elderly inhabitants; however, a handful of Hares emerged. Finn Donnelly Shifted to his human self and scooped up one of them.

Bree, his wife. Jordan remembered reading a report on her.

But Maddie Hunter, Griffin's Mate, was nowhere among the Witch Hares.

Which explains why Griffin's not here either.

At the risk of enraging the Dragon, Jordan interrupted the reunion. "Ash, Bree? Where are the others? What's going on?"

As he'd feared, Bree Donnelly pointed up at the rocks towering over the town. "A small plane crashed into the Cauldron. That's the little pond up there. It took out the wards, the magical container, we'd built around Nemagorix's gate."

Not the most subtle way to destroy a spell... but effective. Sometimes, brute force was good enough.

The Witch Hare's face was deathly pale beneath her flaming crown of hair. "A half dozen Hares from Sedona were up there when it hit. Maddie and a couple of the others ran to see if there were survivors. We were grabbing supplies, hoping to rebuild the wards, when one of the locals spotted the Fangs coming. So, we hid here, in this old root cellar."

Confused, Jordan stared at the trap door. It wasn't *that* subtle. Why hadn't the Fangs discovered them?

Probably didn't care about a bunch of old Navajo.

He hoped. Because the other explanation was scarier.

Maybe they wanted to threaten those Mates. It's the only way to summon the Shifters of the Aegis here.

Reluctantly, Donnelly let his wife slip from his arms. "So, if I'm hearing you right, babe, we need to head up into that mess."

Tears brightened her eyes, but Bree nodded. "I hate to say this, but I think the gate is shattered."

"Yep." Donnelly squinted up at the thunderstorm looming above their heads. "That does look like a demon lord on a rampage, doesn't it? Think we've got a hell of a fight on our hands... no pun intended. You guys are on the spot now. Time to figure out what your damned Aegis does."

CHAPTER 18

To Jordan's shame, the Dragons took charge.

Hurricane-force winds screamed down the ravine that led to the Cauldron, the dank pool at the heart of the rocks above Stillwater. The site where the veil between the worlds grew thin and Nemagorix sought to claw its way into this realm. Rather than face that pandemonium, they chose an aerial assault.

He *should* have been able to help with that. Instead, he had to bite his tongue and be carried in Briggs' claws, like a helpless kitten. Lily, in the other claw, glowed with excitement. For Jordan, though, it was just more proof of how far he'd fallen.

Up they rose, skirting the storm. Once they cleared the high stones, both Dragons drove straight into the tempest.

The first gust flipped Briggs and sent him spinning through the air. Black wings flailed as he fought for control, and suddenly, Jordan found he had no appetite for brooding. Survival was the only thing that mattered now. To him, anyway. Lily cackled with mad glee, like a girl on her first rollercoaster.

To their right, Donnelly fought to conquer the wind by sheer, brute force. Briggs sought a different path. He yielded to the storm, rode it like a crow gliding through a squall. With his passengers, he spun and swirled. Seeking – and finding – the gaps in that wall of wind. The currents of air that drew them naturally inward.

Thus, he was the first to break through to the calm eye at the heart of the chaos.

One moment, Jordan was tossed about like a dish rag in a washer. Then, the air stilled, Briggs righted himself…

And the Worm looked down on their true foes.

A sea of monstrosities filled the little glen. Mangy red lions with black bat wings. Rock statues that lumbered around the pond blindly. Bent human forms, like half-melted wax effigies. Throughout them, inky blobs slithered. Dark-born, seeking mortal hosts to possess.

Above it all, rose a shimmering curtain thirty feet tall. A tear between the worlds. Through it, he caught a glimpse of the black sky and barren stones of Nemagorix's realm.

On the other side, an army waited. Thousands more of these monsters, anxious for their chance to enter this world.

Jordan's stomach roiled at the sight.

Why are they just milling about? We can't stop that many creatures. They should be able to overrun us.

Crimson smears stained the rising stones, and the ground was littered with winged corpses. That explained half the problem.

Those lion-things aren't strong enough to make it through the storm. Every one that tries to fly out of here gets smashed against the canyon walls. No surprise, I guess. Two Dragons barely made it in.

"Why the hell is Nemagorix penning up its own troops?" Jordan yelled.

In Marakeen, the old tongue of Dragons, Briggs shouted

back, "This storm is not the demon's doing. The spirits of this world seek to hold him back."

If so, they were doing a damned fine job. Except... couldn't the demons simply crawl down the path?

Worried, he glanced at the rift in the stones, and saw the slender thread by which the world's fate hung.

Three Hares knelt at the edge of the trail. One, he recognized: Maddie Hunter, Griffin's Mate. The Chimera knelt behind her, his face wracked by agony.

Jordan understood how much it hurt to watch your Mate brave dangers you could do nothing about. The exquisite pain of being unable to protect her.

A tiny line of salt closed off access to the path. Though a hurricane raged around them, not a hair on the Witches' heads stirred as they knelt, palms on the ground. He didn't know a lot about magic, but he knew a ward when he saw one. A magical barrier that kept otherworldly entities at bay.

This one, though, had no runes or spells to lend it power. Only the will of the Hares kept Nemagorix's army at bay, and the strain of that battle showed. Blood trickled from Maddie's nose, staining her shirt a bright red.

She can't hold on much longer. We need to finish this.

Briggs and Donnelly landed behind the wards with their passengers.

"Guys, I'm sorry," Griffin whispered, "I couldn't–"

Jordan waved him silent. No one expected a Shifter to abandon his Mate. "Game time. We've got to figure out this damned Aegis, now. Any ideas?"

"Let's start with the basics." Lucas pulled out the little shield and held it up. "Why don't we all put our hands on it and order Nemagorix to piss off?"

Sounded silly as hell, but he couldn't think of anything else. One by one, Jordan, Briggs, Fairburn, and Griffin, placed a hand on the Aegis.

The Chimera was the last. "Now, whuh…"

The moment the last man's fingers touched the shield, the world vanished. Sky darkened, wind died… and they found themselves standing in a ring of standing stones.

In Nemagorix's realm.

Jordan was the first to speak. "All right. I'm not sure how that was helpful, but at least we managed to get the Aegis to do something."

Slim and elegant, the rune-carved stones were the sole piece of beauty in this demented world. About a half mile away, a black tower rose into the air.

"That's Nemagorix's lair." Griffin, the only one who'd been here before, pointed at it. "There's a big room at the top with a bunch of magicky stuff in it."

Not the most precise explanation the Worm had ever heard. Dammit, why couldn't the Aegis have picked a Hare? "Any idea what it does?"

"Maddie said it looked like a magical prison, but it was broken."

"All right. As a working hypothesis, let's assume that the Aegis fixes it."

Better than nothing, for they were running completely blind. At least that gave them a goal.

There was only one other problem: The rearguard of Nemagorix's army lay between them and the tower… and their arrival hadn't gone unnoticed. The first of those leather-winged lions turned toward them, sniffing the air.

Lucas nudged Fairburn. "Hey, remember how we got the Aegis to glow with just four of us? Since we've got five now, I bet this stupid thing will do a lot more than keep demons away."

This thing offered a form of portable warding? For the

first time, Jordan felt his spirit rise. "Great idea. What do we do?"

"Picture energy running from you to the Aegis," the Wolf replied.

Why did magic always feel like playing make-believe? Feeling ridiculous, he and the other Shifters obeyed. Nothing seemed to happen.

To them. But a bright light burst from the Aegis and two of the drawings on its face twitched. The inky forms of a Bear and Wolf stretched, shimmered… and then leaped off the shield. The Wolf rocketed straight into the air and disappeared. The Bear hovered above them, creating a golden canopy of bright light that covered all five of the Shifters.

"Uh, guys?" Fairburn scowled at the Aegis. "This thing is now stuck to my hand."

"Congratulations, Rex." Jordan clapped him on the back. "It looks like you've been picked to be the porter."

Lucas still stared at the sky above them. "Why did my Wolf take a runner?"

"No idea," Jordan replied. "Let's see if we can move this Bear-shell."

Turned out, they could. The globe of light centered on the Bear. Where Fairburn went, it went, and as long as the others kept close, it covered them all. Despite the uneven ground, the group jogged toward the tower. A decent pace that made Jordan's spirits rise.

Until they met the first enemy.

One of the bat-winged lions swooped down. When it hit the edge of the Aegis' radiance, it careened off, screeching in pain. But Fairburn stopped too, with a soft grunt.

"I felt that," he muttered. "It's like I'm carrying a glass ball around us."

Oh, hell. Did that mean…? "Is the glass cracking?"

"No. But I'm going to have a hell of a time 'pushing' it

through that." He pointed at the sea of hideous creatures roiling toward them.

"Well, do your best." What other choice did they have?

Two more flying monstrosities pinged off their shield. Then, the edge of the tide arrived.

Darkborn swept across the ground, swirling along the edges of the light. Black steam hissed off them where they touched it, and yet, they still came. Hundreds of them. A river of filth seeking a crack in their defenses. Behind that, man-shaped rock piles stomped up. Their punches never dented the dome of light that protected the Shifters. Yet, the strain of defending it showed on the Bear's face. Sweat began to trickle down Fairburn's cheeks. His breathing slowed, and so did his pace. From a jog to a walk, and then to a crawl.

Finally, they stopped completely. Surrounded by screaming monsters. Still a quarter mile away from Nemagorix's tower.

"Fairburn?" Jordan kept his voice calm, even though he raged inside.

"Sorry," the Bear panted. "Can't."

"Dammit, try harder!" Griffin snarled.

The Worm laid a hand on his arm, though he couldn't blame the man. The only thing holding Nemagorix back was his Mate, Maddie. She couldn't take much more of this. If they didn't bind the demon lord soon, she would die.

And thousands of people with her.

Yelling didn't help, though. "Anyone got any bright ideas?"

"I can breathe fire ahead of us," Briggs offered. "Try to clear a path."

"Sounds like a plan. Why don't you—"

High above, a howl echoed in the dark skies.

The Wolf from the Aegis shot down in a streak of silver, sliding nimbly through the swarm of bat-lions circling above them. As it hit the edge of their shield, it vanished, and the dome of light grew brighter.

From the heavens, a single horn answered that howl with a clear, sharp note. More joined it. Dozens… hundreds…

Then the sky split, and light spilled forth.

Hundreds of winged horses plummeted from the dusk, their white feathers gleaming. Each bore a rider armored in bright silver. Armed as well, for a rain of glittering arrows showered down around them. Every one that touched a demon, killed.

For a moment, all five Shifters gaped at this new army. "Okay," Lucas finally said. "I think my Wolf ran to get the cavalry."

One Pegasus swooped low overhead. The Shifters scrambled to one side and the horse touched down neatly in the space they cleared, not a feather outside of the Aegis' protection.

Close now, Jordan could get a better view of the rider. He was a fey, delicate man with violet eyes and pale hair. Tall and thin, too beautiful to be human.

Adanai? He'd read reports on the fairy-like creatures that ruled the Other Side. He'd never seen one, though.

Well, courtesy never went wrong. "Thank you," he told the strange warrior. "We could use your help."

The rider ignored him. Instead, he bowed to a startled Lucas Clay. "The Call has been heard and answered. The promise made shall be fulfilled."

"Uh… okay?" The Wolf backed to the edge of the light and glanced about at his companions.

Not that they could help him. The Adanai refused to even look at the other Shifters. "You're up, Clay," Jordan grumbled. "Talk to the man."

"If you need nothing more, I shall join my brothers in the battle and—"

"No! Wait!" the Wolf yipped. "We need information."

The rider settled back in his saddle. "Ask."

"Who are you, what's the Call, what's the promise, and how do we lock up Nemagorix?"

That was one way to get it all out there. Jordan bit back a chuckle as the Adanai cocked his head in confusion. "Do you not know anything?"

"Basically… no."

"Yet you *are* the Handmaiden's son. I see her in your visage."

"My mom died when I was born. I got nothing – except the Aegis."

Griffin tapped his wrist, as if checking a clock. Lucas nodded and added, "We've got to hurry, but if you could fill us in quickly."

"You are the son of the Queen's Handmaiden. The Lords of the Banner promised her that if she could recover the Aegis, we would aid her – or her chosen – when she sought to chain the Enemy."

"You're all Adanai, right?" The warrior nodded. "So, my Wolf called you and you're here to protect us. Cool. So, uh, how do we bind this creep?"

"Return the Aegis to the Guardians at the top of the tower."

Lucas repeated the plan carefully. "You get these demons off our back. We walk to the tower. Hand the Aegis over to the Guardians and they do the rest. Got it."

Simple enough. But the plan didn't make any sense to Jordan. "Hang on. You say the Handmaiden 'recovered' the Aegis. From where?" The Adanai ignored him once more, and he sighed. "Lucas, could you ask him that?"

When the Wolf repeated his exact words, the rider deigned to answer. "From the Guardians, I assume."

That was *not* good... "If she was right there with the Aegis, why didn't she just hand it back to them?"

Silence. Until Lucas played 'translator.'

"I don't know."

Great. "Another question, if you would, Lucas. If the Aegis was with the Guardians, why wasn't it binding Nemagorix?"

To his surprise, the rider actually had an answer to that. "The thousand years had passed. Their aid must be requested every millennium."

"And the Handmaiden didn't ask... because?"

"I don't know. Perhaps she could not persuade them."

Uneasy, Jordan glanced around their little circle. "Anyone got a clue about how to 'persuade' spirits?"

Briggs volunteered at once. "I am familiar with the rituals that show respect to Earth spirits. I would imagine they also please the spirits of this realm."

"Don't rites require things? Knives, sage, tobacco... other ceremonial items?" The Dragon nodded at him. "Where are we going to get all of that?"

"In my pouch." Briggs patted a bag at his side.

Griffin snorted. "Do I dare ask why you carry that stuff around all the time?"

"In case I need to appease a spirit," the Dragon said. Like that ought to be obvious to everyone.

"All right," Jordan chuckled. "Briggs, you get a merit badge. Lucas, order your army to clear a path for us. Let's get this show on the road."

At the Wolf's command, the Adanai's mount leaped into the air. Rains of arrows quickly mowed down the enemies before them. Once more, Fairburn could push ahead.

Onward, they staggered. Running over Darkborn. Rocked on their heels whenever one of the walking stone piles collided with them. Throughout it all, Fairburn drove the group forward. Drenched in sweat and panting… but a Bear to the end. A man who protected his companions with his life, if necessary.

Finally, the tower loomed before them, a sliver of inky blackness in the eternal twilight of this place. The monsters fell back, as if even they were frightened to approach Nemagorix too closely. Ahead, an open doorway gaped like a toothless mouth. They tottered toward it…

And bounced off, repelled by some invisible barrier.

"What the hell?" Fairburn gasped, his sides heaving.

As if in answer to his question, a reedy voice whispered from the doorway. "My master has sealed the way. None may pass without his blessing."

Jordan studied the sweat-drenched Bear. "Think you're strong enough to try to hammer this thing down?"

"Don't know but I'll try," Fairburn promised.

Before he could, Griffin held up a hand. "Back us around the corner. I may have an easier solution."

Good thing, because Jordan wasn't sure they *could* punch their way into the demon lord's home.

Once out of sight of the door, the Chimera whispered, "Magical guardians often aren't very smart – at least, in the stories. Let me see if I can trick this one."

On all sides, Adanai and demons fought, locked in a mortal struggle. Griffin waited until the tide of the war swung away from them… and then, he stepped outside of the Aegis' protective shell. Before Jordan could shout a warning, he collapsed. In the blink of an eye, a mouse stood where once there had been a man.

Its tiny nose twitched, its whiskers shivered, as the little creature concentrated. Then, a fountain of black smoke erupted from the ground. It billowed twenty feet above the ground, and eyes opened within it. Burning red eyes, glowing with malevolence.

Nemagorix.

Jordan's mouth went dry as he considered the Chimera's bluff. At the last defense of Stillwater, the man saw the demon lord and heard it speak. In theory, he could mimic any creature he knew. But if this disguise wasn't perfect... "Listen, at the first sign that they aren't falling for it, come back!"

Griffin swept past them, gliding with complete confidence up to the doorway. "Open!" he shouted.

Jordan's breath caught in his throat... until that thin voice warbled, "As my master commands."

"Allow these vermin in too," the Chimera said as he drifted inside. Like the good, dutiful, mindless servant it was, the guardian of the gate let them pass as well.

The moment they were through the doorway, Griffin Shifted back and leaped within the Aegis' protective glow. "Yay for idiot guards," he muttered. "This way, Fairburn. I've been here before and I know where to find Nemagorix."

Up, he led them. Through echoing corridors and stairs. Nothing – demon or living – awaited them. At the very top, Griffin led the men into a vast chamber. Barren, stark, with neither furniture nor decorations beneath its vaulted ceiling. At one end, lay a black dais.

Empty as well. Griffin glanced about uneasily. "Last time I was here, Nemagorix stood on that thing."

Jordan eyed the large expanse of nothingness that surrounded them. "I don't see any guardians."

Casey Briggs knew the answer to that puzzle. "You would not see a spirit unless it wished to present itself. Let me introduce us."

The Dragon knelt at the edge of the light. From his satchel, he withdrew a handful of small pouches, each one full of the oddest things. Tobacco and red ochre paint. Several sage smudge sticks. A gourd rattle decorated with red and black lines. Arranging them before himself, he began to sing in a language Jordan didn't recognize.

Hope to hell these spirits know Navajo or Hopi or whatever the hell that is...

Then again, they'd understood English just fine. Clearly, he didn't understand the first thing about speaking to spirits. Nothing good happened when ignorant people gave orders, so the Worm shut up and let the expert do his job.

For several minutes, nothing happened. Briggs droned on, sharp rattles interspersed among his words. Griffin twitched with impatience as the delay grew. Each moment was a threat, a dagger aimed at the heart of his Mate, and the Chimera was near his breaking point. At last, though, two rough human forms faded into view. Eight feet tall, with small bull horns and dull red skin. And flat! More like walking pictures than living creatures.

The Dragon bowed his head to the strange beings. "Greetings to you, Guardians of the Darkness. You honor us with your presence."

"Greetings to you, Bearers of the Aegis. What would you have of us?"

Now, for the big question: Would they bind Nemagorix? Was it, in the end, going to be that simple?

"Elders, we ask that you take up the Aegis once more and lock Nemagorix away from the world of mortal men."

"We accept this burden for a thousand years."

"Sweet!" Lucas gave a quick fist pump.

Perhaps it was his paranoia, the long, depressing years he'd lived as a Worm, but Jordan couldn't share the Wolf's excitement. The story of the Handmaiden still left him uneasy. "Briggs, could you ask the Guardians why the Handmaiden didn't ask them to do this?"

Fortunately, these creatures – unlike the Adanai – didn't suffer from selective deafness. One of them answered him directly. "She did so request, and we agreed. But she could not walk the Gauntlet."

And there it was: The hidden catch. "What's the Gauntlet."

"That." One papery hand waved toward the black dais. "You must place the Aegis in its center. It will draw Nemagorix back and hold him here."

Lucas eyed the Guardians with open suspicion. "That's, like, a ten-foot walk. Why couldn't Mom pull it off?"

"Nemagorix does not wish you to pass, and the Aegis shields only your bodies, not your souls."

"What happens if we try to walk the Gauntlet and fail?" Jordan asked.

"Then the Aegis will shatter in your hands, as it shattered in hers. And you will be driven from this realm."

Back into their own world. But, unlike Lucas' parents, *they* would get to see their home destroyed. Nemagorix had spent the last couple of decades destroying all the bars of his prison.

Except one. The Aegis.

"Guess this is it, then." Jordan gazed about the circle at his brothers in arms. Four strangers who'd trusted him, despite his flaws. "I'd like to give some rousing speech, but I think Griffin would strangle me if I slowed us down any more."

"Let me add one request," Briggs said. "If I fall, leave me. One of us must make it to the center or the world ends."

"Same," Lucas chimed in, as the others nodded. "All that matters is, locking Nemagorix back up."

Jordan closed his eyes and drew a deep breath. The image that came to him wasn't his pathetic excuse of a life. It was Savannah. The light that had led him out of the darkness. He might be a Worm, a loathsome, fallen Dragon. But he had won the love of a good woman. A true Mate. He would do this for her.

And, if he died, he prayed she'd understand.

Together, they approached the Gauntlet. One shared look, one murmur of 'Good luck,' and they stepped across the threshold together.

Darkness swallowed them. The room vanished, devoured by a cyclone of screaming voices. They boomed in Jordan's head, driving all rational thought from his mind. Men and women, children and elders. All screaming in horror.

Of him. Of his shame and crimes.

The face of his first love whirled by, tears streaming down her face. "You left me!" she wailed. "You never really loved me!" A child's terrified cries joined her: "Papa, where are you? Papa, why can't I find you?" One after another, all his sins joined them. The people he'd killed. The innocents he'd failed. An endless parade of guilt and remorse.

One he knew very well.

There wasn't a single face there that he hadn't seen in his dreams. No new hauntings. No fresh sins he'd forgotten. He recognized the Voice of the Gauntlet like an old, bitter friend.

Around him, the other Shifters rocked, faces ashen. "Come on," he called, praying they could hear him through the onslaught of guilt the Gauntlet poured on them. "Keep moving!"

Jordan stepped forward. Lucas, Griffin, and Fairburn staggered on as well. But Briggs dropped to his knees.

"This isn't right," the wide-eyed Dragon hissed. "I have failed. I haven't done the rites properly. I don't know what to say. I give insult."

Fairburn tugged at him, but the man seemed glued to the ground. In the end, they left him, as he'd wished.

A deed that shook Jordan to his core.

He was the best of us. If he can't make it, what hope do we have?

Two steps later, Fairburn crumbled, weeping about his first Mate, a woman he'd failed to save. Jordan scooped the Aegis from his hands; this time, the little shield did not resist.

Halfway there, Lucas dissolved into howls. "Ash, I'm so sorry. I'm such an idiot. I am so, so sorry."

White as a sheet, Griffin tried to force a smile as the two of them wobbled forward. "Just us assholes now."

Ghosts shrieked of Jordan's crimes, a litany of guilt that threatened to drown him. Yet, a strange emotion threaded its way into the ocean of shame, and the Worm clung to it like a life preserver.

Annoyance.

He was *irritated*.

Seriously, Briggs? You're devastated because... you were rude?!? A trivial 'sin' like that doesn't even make it on my list! And Lucas and Fairburn failed once? Ha! Try a dozen times. Try a score of times. One measly sin does you in? Damn, you should try being a Worm!

Shielded by his growing anger, he marched on. Wrath wrapped him in a blanket, a warmth that kept his guilt at bay. He barely noticed when Griffin dropped, moaning about what a monster he was. Idiots. They didn't even know what that word meant!

I do. Like you, I know.

Cold as a serpent's kiss, those words slid into Jordan's mind.

The darkness faded away. He found himself lulled into motionless torpor only five feet from the dais' center.

Ahead, Nemagorix stood. A cloud of pure hatred and greed. Eyes of molten gold seemed to peer into his very soul. Tasting, savoring, the ruin he'd made of his life.

I know what it means to be a monster, the demon lord whispered. *I would honor you for the magnitude of your crimes.*

"I don't want your 'honor,'" he snapped. His foot seemed

to weigh a thousand pounds now, but he raised it and took a step forward.

You are not so different from me. Join me. Serve me, and I will place the world at your feet.

"I don't want the world. And I'm not like you." A second step.

Face your accusers. Black ropes lashed out, pointing at his ghosts. *Tell* them *you are not like me.*

"I have." Halfway there. "I face them every night." A symphony of screams and wails filled the chamber, until the air was a solid mass of accusation. One more step. Just one more...

Look at your fellows! Was that a touch of panic in the demon lord's voice? *How can a Worm like you succeed where they have failed?*

Finally, Jordan understoond, and he laughed. "I will succeed *because* I am a Worm. That's why the Aegis chose me. Alone, of all of them, I know what a wretch I am."

Then you know you are unworthy!

"Yes. But it doesn't matter."

Because she loved him. Savannah. She had looked upon the rancid mess he'd made of his soul... and she still loved him.

She saw hope where he found only despair.

He would do this for her.

With the last ounce of his strength, Jordan Beaumont fell forward.

And placed the Aegis at the heart of the Gauntlet.

CHAPTER 19

'Victory' brought no joy. In fact, Savannah couldn't force herself to think of the day's events that way. As the sun set over Stillwater, the black sky overhead matched the darkness in her heart.

The gate to Nemagorix's realm closed shortly after the Shifters of the Aegis disappeared. Yet no one celebrated, for none of the men had returned. They were either dead or trapped in that hellish realm with the demon they bound. Closing the portal had been their final act of sacrifice.

"Can't you open it just a crack?" she'd begged Maddie Hunter. "Maybe they're just on the other side. If we could help them escape…"

Bloody and exhausted from her magical battles, the Witch Hare fought back tears. Griffin, her Mate, was one of the lost men. "I'm sorry, but no. Whatever they did locked the gate from the other side. It can't be opened from our world. It's shut… tight."

That last word trailed off, and Savannah knew why. It was the final, terrible failure of their 'victorious' day.

The gate to Nemagorix's realm *wasn't* sealed tight. Oh, it

was immobile, impossible to open. It gave them no way to rescue their loved ones. Yet, a thin trickle of dark magic seeped through the Cauldron. A thread of energy, a hint of corruption, that proved the gate was not completely closed.

Jordan and the others had given their lives, and Savannah wasn't sure their sacrifice had won anything.

Out in the desert, a fire blazed bright against the night sky. Donnelly had gathered the dead Fangs. Far away from the town, he incinerated their bodies, cleansing the land with Dragon fire. Only six shrouded corpses remained. The Hares who'd been at the Cauldron when the plane crashed. They, however, would be taken home and given proper honors and burial.

Smaller lights flickered in the dark, and soon, the distant roar of engines joined them.

An army of motorcycles rumbled up the track that led to Stillwater. All three Packs – Sand, Sage, and Big River – had come to pay their respects. Aaron King led the way.

When his bike rolled to a stop, a slender woman with brown curls leaped from behind him. She tore her helmet off to reveal a tear-stained, furious face. The moment she spotted Lily, she charged her.

"Omega…" The Wolf held up a hand. The newcomer threw her helmet as hard as she could, and Lily didn't even try to dodge.

"Screw you, King!" she screamed. "Screw you! You promised you'd never leave me behind! You *liar!*"

Oh, hell. Savannah knew who she must be. Paige Fairburn. Rex's Mate.

"Omega, I couldn't come get you. It happened too fast. You can't tell a Dragon to swing by Colorado before he rescues his Mate."

"Rex is *my* Mate! My Mate is gone too, and I… I didn't…"

The rest of her words vanished in a sob as the young

woman's strength crumbled. With a wail, Paige collapsed to the ground, tears pouring forth. Lily lowered herself to the dust beside her and pulled her friend into a hug. Gently, she rocked, her grief spilling forth for all to see.

Around them, the Wolves held silent vigil. They were a wild and fiercely joyful Kind. Yet, they understood loss and pain, and they honored it.

Gradually, Paige's sobs grew less ragged. When her tears finally slowed, Lily pulled away. "You *are* part of the Pack, Omega. I will always bring you – if I can."

"I know," Paige sniffed. "I'm sorry. I–"

"Shut up." Lily gave her a playful punch in the shoulder. "Never apologize to a Wolf for nipping her. She probably had it coming. Now, let's round up the Pack and save our Mates' dumb asses."

"What?" That sudden announcement set Savannah's head spinning. "Do you think we can?"

Lily brushed the dirt from her riding leathers as she rose. "We're gonna try."

"Are they even alive?" Paige scrubbed her face clean of tears and followed her friend.

"If they aren't, I plan to get their bodies back. I'm giving Casey a proper funeral."

Heavens, how could the Wolf even say that? The thought of burying Jordan... of going through the rest of her life without him... was too terrible for Savannah.

They swung by the shack where Maddie rested, and the Hare joined their little group. Names were passed, hands shaken. Then, silence fell as they hiked along the battered path that led up to the Cauldron.

A few Witches remained, struggling to make sense of this half-closed, untouchable gate. One was Ash Anderson, Lucas' Mate. A feverish gleam burned in her brown eyes as she scrambled over to their little group. "Our Mates aren't dead. I can feel them. They're here, and they're alive."

As a psychic, she'd know better than anyone. Yet, her revelation didn't cheer Savannah as much as it should.

If we can't free our Mates, that's almost worse. They'll die slowly.

Maddie, their one true Witch, stepped to the water's edge. "Has there been any change?"

"No."

"Any idea how to crack this door open? Or, hell, why it's not fully closed?"

"None."

So, here they were, right back at the problem. Clueless again. Savannah balled her fists, choking with fury at her helplessness.

Lily, always unsinkable, stepped to Maddie's side. "Time to brainstorm then. The portal's in the middle of this pool, right?" When the Hare nodded, so did she. "Great. Let's try the obvious answer first."

Without warning, the Wolf dashed into the water and threw herself, headfirst, through its center. She sailed past the gate's location… and plunged into the water.

Nothing happened. A moment later, she picked herself up, sputtering and soaked. "Okay, you can't just walk in."

Yet, a slight frown creased her brow, and Savannah noticed that she walked *around* the former gate, not through it. "Are you all right, Lily?"

"Yeah." The Wolf bit her lip.

"Nonsense. What's wrong?"

"It's nothing. Just…" All the other Mates stared at her, and the biker blushed. "I just thought I kind of felt Casey when I jumped into the pond, laughing at me for trying to bull rush a spirit door."

That was all they needed to hear. All the women rushed forward, stumbling on the Cauldron's slick stones.

Savannah raised her hands before her, reaching into the air.

A hint of warmth brushed against her skin. So slight, so faint, that she thought her mind played tricks on her.

Until Ash squeaked with delight. "You're right! I can feel Lucas! He's here, and he's fine!"

But *still* trapped.

None of this helped. This didn't get them any closer to opening the portal.

Unless…

What if they were asking the wrong question?

"Maddie, this door, it's the Aegis, isn't it? It's the thing that stops them from coming home."

"I… well, yes," the Hare admitted. "I hadn't thought of it like that, but yes, the Aegis is the actual protective barrier."

"Then can't it decide to let them through?" Savannah asked. "I mean, it's not some mindless relic. It chose our Mates. Doesn't that mean it's intelligent? If we ask it—"

Lily's bellow made them all jump. "GIVE ME BACK MY MATE, YOU SHITTY LITTLE SHIELD!"

No Mates appeared.

Paige coughed. "Maybe manners count? Um, dear Aegis, please let my Mate Rex come back to me."

Again, no result, and Maddie sighed. "I don't think this will work. We can't make the Aegis do anything. It chose them, not us."

And they Chose us, as Mates. Doesn't that matter?

Something nagged at Savannah. Words, half-forgotten. Something she'd heard… where? At a wedding?

For this cause shall a man leave his father and mother, and shall be joined unto his wife, that they two shall be one flesh.

"Oh…," she breathed. "I know why the gate won't close. It

can't! We're standing in it! Don't you see? We're not thinking about this right! Can you shut a door if someone's stuck their arm through the doorway?"

Lily wrinkled her nose, face scrunched up in concentration. "Maybe."

"No, you can't," Paige growled. "Not without breaking the door."

Trust the other Bear Kin to see her point. "Exactly! It wouldn't close properly."

Maddie rubbed her temples. "I understand your analogy, but what does that have to do with this gate?"

"Don't you remember what they say in marriages? 'That they two shall be one flesh'? What if that's not just words? What if it's true, spiritually?"

Around her, hope brightened the faces of the other women, and Savannah felt her own spirit soar. "When Jordan Claimed me... when I accepted that... I bound myself to him for all time. I'm not just 'Savannah Dare' anymore. I'm Jordan's Mate. We're linked. And I think that," she jabbed a finger at the invisible gate, "can't sever our link."

"So, it's like Casey's the hand and I'm the shoulder...," Lily started.

"...and there's a connection between you..."

"...an arm..." The Wolf seemed determined to take her literally.

"...that the Aegis can't, or won't, sever."

"Can we just pull them through, then?" Paige asked.

Maddie shook her head. "I don't know any way to physically grab magic."

But, sometimes, knowledge was a hindrance, not a help. The Hare's training said this was impossible? Savannah's heart refused to believe that.

She raised her hands in the air, palms out. Seeking that hint, that gentle touch, she'd felt before.

There! Soft as a kitten's fur, she felt it.

Jordan's hands pressed against hers.

Savannah curled her fingers, seeking to weave them through his. It was like trying to grab mist, and for a second, she feared Maddie was right. Jordan was a spirit now, impossible for her to touch.

Then call his spirit.

Call his Dragon.

She remembered the great serpent lying, forgotten and decaying, at the bottom of that dream pond. How it had pulled itself to the surface to save her. Talons that could shred steel wrapped gently about her body, leaving not a single bruise behind.

Beneath her fingers, the air grew cool and hard. Like a Dragon's scales.

Now, the man.

Jordan. Once master, now Mate. Even as an 'enemy', he had fought to protect her from every threat, whether Dark-born or simply an angry, arrogant Wolf. His love – hot and true – had burned away the cobwebs that Todd wove in her mind. No longer would she accept table scraps of affection from any man. Jordan had shown her love, true love. Passion and ecstasy. She was his strength, he her delight. Together, they would heal his Dragon and build a future together.

'Scales' softened and grew warm to the touch. Gently, she twined her fingers through them. And this time, *this time*, she felt his hand in hers.

Gasps rang out as she pulled him toward her. The fabric of the gate bent, curved…

But would not break. Jordan was still trapped.

"Help me," she begged.

Four women leaped forward. Four pairs of palms pressed against the air.

"Think of your Mate's spirit, and how much you love him."

Four faces scrunched in furious concentration.

"Now, bring them back."

Fingers linked. Hands pulled.

And then, five dusty, bloody Shifters came tumbling back into the real world.

ow was the time for true celebration.

Once the Mates were reunited, the portal closed – just as Savannah had guessed. Fully, completely… and for a thousand years. Neither they, their children, nor their grandchildren need ever fear Nemagorix again.

Five pairs of lovers strolled down to Stillwater. Each one lost in their own private bliss.

Tucked beneath Jordan's arm, Savannah basked in his admiration. "The best Hares on the West Coast were baffled… and *you* figured it out! I watched the whole thing. We could actually watch you all through that damned portal."

What a horrible death that would have been! Trapped in a hellish world, tormented by visions of your home. Inches away… yet unreachable.

She couldn't bear to think of that. Savannah pushed the thought out of her mind.

As they walked, the men explained what had happened. How they'd locked up the demon lord. How Nemagorix's forces had fled, scattered by the Adanai warriors.

"Hang on!" Lily bristled with outrage. "Those guys didn't just fly off and leave you behind, did they?"

"Yeah, they did," her brother grumbled. "That is *exactly* what they did."

"What a bunch of dicks!" the Wolf squawked.

"Lily...," Briggs sighed.

"Don't you 'Lily' me, bud! We're gonna figure out how to get to Adanai-Land, and then, I'm going to kick some serious ass."

Back in town, laughter and love enveloped them. Real celebration, heart-felt and wild, broke out. Tossed by the waves of celebration, the couples drifted apart. Griffin and Maddie joined the elderly Navajo that he knew so well. The Fairburns ended up chatting with the Donnellys and Hares. Meanwhile, Briggs, Lily, Ash and Lucas all got dragged into a three-Pack squabble about which Wolves had to make the long, dusty ride back to town... to pick up beer. Briggs volunteered, but Lily insisted the only proper way to settle the issue was a massive arm-wrestling competition.

With no one to demand their attention, Savannah and Jordan wandered to the edge of town, seeking a bit of peace. There, looking up at the star-filled sky, she kissed him again.

"I am so proud of you."

"All of us share the credit," he protested but still accepted her adoring kiss.

"You were the only one who could walk the Gauntlet, though."

"Poor Nemagorix didn't stand a chance. I've spent decades brooding over my failings. It couldn't tell me anything I didn't already know. I guess that's the benefit of being a Worm. Who knew there was one?"

He meant it as a joke, she knew, but Savannah still pinched him. "You're not a Worm. You're an injured Dragon."

"Same thing."

Could he not see how much he'd changed? "No, they're not. A Worm doesn't care about his sins. Only a Dragon does."

"All right." A quick kiss on her nose was her reward. "I see your point."

"Plus, you didn't give up. That's the amazing part. You knew everything you'd done – and you kept trying. You didn't give in to despair."

"Because of you." He stared off into the desert, suddenly unwilling to meet her gaze. "You looked on the mess I'd made of my soul and you still loved me."

His own words seemed to worry him, for he suddenly turned and peered into her eyes. "You do love me, yes?"

"Of course. Silly." Savannah snuggled against him, and felt his reserve, his nerves, melt away.

"And you'll stay with me?"

"Forever." It was a promise that needed no thought.

"You understand I'm a wreck, right? It will be a long time before my Dragon heals."

"And I'll be at your side for all of it." Nursing him back to spiritual health was a 'chore' she would take up gleefully.

"Good. I promise I will marry you as soon as I'm well."

"What!" she yelped. "Why on Earth would we wait that long?"

"I'm not well. You know that…"

"So? The vows say, 'in sickness *and* in health', remember?"

"But…"

"'For better, for worse'…?"

Jordan winced. "Normally, people start with the 'better' part."

"So, we do it backwards. Who cares?"

She expected him to laugh. Instead, he studied her face, baffled and delighted. "Truly? You'd marry me now?"

"Now. As you are. Pop the question, if you don't believe me."

"Tomorrow," he promised. "I'll ask you tomorrow."

"Again, with the delays! Why not now?"

Jordan held up his empty hand. "I don't have a ring."

Savannah pursed her lips, eyeing him up and down with mock displeasure. "Okay. *That* I'm willing to wait for. But only a day. Promise?"

"I promise."

And then, he kissed her.

The years would be full of challenges. She didn't doubt them or fear them. No matter how far the road to redemption stretched, they would walk it together. Man and woman, Dragon and Mate. Love would be their beacon, their strength, as they built their own future.

* * *

Thank you for reading Alpha Protector Dragon...and hopefully the full 11 Books Wellsprings series! If you haven't read the Dragon Dreams series (that proceeds the Shifters of the Aegis series) please go check it out! Otherwise we have another series from Cynthia Wilde that we think you will like! Her Keeper Bear is the first book in the Burning Falls series!

Click here to get Her Keeper Bear on Amazon!

Ok, fine...here is a little preview of Her Keeper Bear...

THE IMAGE IN HER REAR-VIEW MIRROR REFLECTED THE JAGGED New York skyline fading into the distance. The dim, gray color of the sky mirrored Cindy's mood, drizzling large spattering rain drops onto her windshield.

"Good riddance, New York," she muttered as she sped down the two-lane highway. Her time in the city had done her no favors outside of her professional life. More specifically, Reginald Anderson, though he preferred Reggie.

Cindy had fallen for his smooth demeanor, and the fact that he was a co-worker did not deter her from a series of toe-curling dalliances after hours. The affair ended badly. As it turned out, smooth-talking Reggie was having a clandestine romance with another colleague as well.

She found out about his "dalliance" one night when she had to return to work unexpectedly to retrieve a file she needed to go over before a morning meeting. When she got to the office, she spotted his light on down the hall and opted for a surprise pop-in.

"Hi, Reggie," Cindy had purred as she opened his door. She found him between the thighs of his personal assistant, her bare backside perched on the shelf of his bookcase which was rattling against the wall as his hips thrust into her with great gusto.

He had not even tried to pretend an apology. "We never said we were exclusive," he called out between gritted teeth, not even pausing his machinations. Cindy absorbed the scene in silence, watching them for a few seconds before she spoke.

"That's okay," she demurred. "I wanted to let you know I'd like to submit my resignation, effective at once. Goodbye Reg."

In three days' time, she managed to pare down her

belongings enough to fit the remainder into the back of her Prius. What she could not cram into her car, she had dropped, without ceremony, to the nearest thrift store. She could not stop herself from chuckling as she drove past the sign indicating the edge of the small town she had once called home.

'The City of Burning Falls Welcomes You!' followed by a small clip art picture of a flame beneath a waterfall. The waterfall itself was far more poetic than the sign would show and the only thing which held any sentimental memories for her from her hometown.

"You are always welcome," her grandmother said. "For as long as you like."

"You might be right, Nan," she had replied. "New York is wonderful, but the city is so fast paced. I think I need a break."

"What aren't you telling me?" Nan replied with a wry tone.

"Why do you ask?" Cindy said, trying to evade the second sense her grandmother always had about her.

"It's that boy, isn't it?"

"Well, Reggie's thirty-five, so I wouldn't call him a boy."

"I knew he was trouble, being so much older than you. It was not a good match."

"Only ten years, Nan. That's not that much older than me. And besides, I wasn't looking for a match. Maybe just a flame."

"I'd like you to come," her grandmother said. "I'm not as young as I used to be, you know."

"Oh, Nan. You're only as young as you feel, as you always point out."

"That's the problem. I don't feel as young as I once did. I'm getting tired more often, these days. It might be nice to have someone else here for a little while. Just in case."

"Okay, fine. If only for a little while."

Cindy and Nan had always had a unique relationship, much to the chagrin of Cindy's parents. Nan had encouraged Cindy's creative endeavors, always asking to see her latest designs, even when she was a child. After high school, she had skipped town as quick as she could blink, taking a job as an intern in New York, which led to a full-time position in the fashion industry. Cindy felt that much of her success came because of Nan's encouragement.

A few minutes after passing the welcome sign, houses began to appear at the edge of the two-lane road. Farmhouses placed back from the road with large, sweeping yards, gravel drives and cute little flower gardens adorning the porches.

"Ah, home," Cindy said, not without some irony in her tone. "New York this is not," she murmured. Soon, she arrived at Nan's house. The nearest neighbor being about a quarter of a mile away, still visible, but from a distance. Cindy smiled as she pulled into the driveway.

Her grandmother's house had always had a certain element of character, compared to the other homes. Besides the lavender hydrangeas planted around the base of the raised porch, she also kept a collection of wind chimes, birdhouses, and painted gourds all over the porch. The house reflected her grandmother's eclectic personality.

Cindy exited the car, hearing the light tinkling sounds as the breeze drifted through the décor, the sounds of childhood. She had not even made it to the front step before the door flung open.

"There you are!" Nan stepped out with arms wide, rushed into the yard and scooped her up into a huge bear hug. "I thought you'd never get here!"

"Hi, Nan," Cindy said.

Nan shuffled her inside before grabbing her suitcase,

carrying it as if it were light as a feather, her long flowered skirt swishing around her sandals. Cindy could not keep from smiling as the woman dragged them both into the house.

"Come in, come in! I've got soup in the crock pot waiting for you. It won't be ready for another hour though. I've got tea. Would you like tea? I can put on the kettle in no time at all." She fluttered around the house, picking and adjusting the already pristine home.

"Tea would be nice." Cindy took a seat at the kitchen table, a relic from a bygone era, made of lime green Formica. The room filled with cheery welcoming scents of the rich chicken broth bubbling in the corner. Within moments, the tea kettle hummed on the stove. Nan poured two cups of hot water over the spiced tea satchels.

"Cream, sugar?" she asked, peering over her shoulder.

"Oh, both please," Cindy replied.

"Ah, it is a 'both' sort of day. Isn't it?" Nan turned and sat down across from her, placing the steaming mug before the young woman. "So, tell me about New York. Is it as glamorous as everyone says?"

Cindy sipped her tea, relishing in the cinnamon and comforting sweetness of the flavors. "Ugh, I've had enough of glamor," she said. "Though I think you should visit the city sometime. You would love it there. It's a wonderful place to visit."

"But you wouldn't want to live there?" Nan laughed.

"Goes without saying," Cindy replied.

"Maybe so," Nan said. "Besides, I think I have enough to contend with here in the 'City of Burning Falls.'"

CONTINUE THE FIRST STORY IN THE BURNING FALLS SHIFTERS series, Her Keeper Bear, here on Amazon…